LIAR LIKE HER

A SECRETS AND LIES SUSPENSE NOVEL

D.L. WOOD

SILVERGLASS
PRESS

ISBN-13: 979-8-5740-7715-3
First edition
Silverglass Press
Huntsville, Alabama

D.L. Wood
www.dlwoodonline.com
Huntsville, Alabama

ACKNOWLEDGMENTS

I want to send a heartfelt thank-you to —

You, my readers, for choosing to spend some of your valuable time in my stories, and allowing me to continue doing what I love.

My incredible, hard-working beta readers: Kimberly Pugh, Kari Long, Tessa Hobbs, Laura Stratton, Kirsten Harbers and Gene Gettler.

My beta reader and technical advisor, Shaw Gookin. You make my books better.

My editor, Lenda Selph. Thank you for your selfless work and relentless attention to detail.

My friend and fellow author, Luana Ehrlich, whose constant encouragement and guidance I treasure.

The women of the Dangerous Deceptions Boxed Set, who have taught me much and become sweet friends.

My parents, Lynn and Bob Plummer, whose never-ending belief in me still is the fuel that feeds the engine.

And Ron, my husband, whose hard work and encouragement make it possible for me to live out my dream of being an author.

For *Manna House-Huntsville*, and *For Life Ministries-Huntsville*, and all the other wonderful, dedicated persons and organizations who work tirelessly to meet the needs of others in this world so that they are not left hungry for either bread or hope.

1

"It isn't possible for three girls to vanish into thin air, Nate." From behind the closed door of her bedroom, twelve-year-old Quinn Bello heard her mother in the hallway, speaking to her father in hushed tones. Her raspy voice quivered, betraying the panic Quinn knew she must be feeling.

Tucked in her bed, Quinn stared at the purple polka-dots on the sheet pulled up over her head. The fresh-linen scent left by the fabric softener filled her nostrils and she breathed it in, trying to calm herself.

Please don't let them come in here.

Please don't let them come in here.

But they did. Her mother shook her, apparently attempting to wake Quinn from what she thought was a deep sleep.

"Quinn, honey, wake up," her mother urged, her delicate fingers grasping Quinn's shoulder.

Quinn ignored her. Lying still, tucked beneath her down duvet in her second-floor bedroom in their house in Seaglass Cove, Florida, she feigned sleep.

Her mother shook her harder. Realizing there was no

avoiding it, Quinn rolled over. "Mom! What?" she groaned, sounding more tired than she was. The rainbow-colored digits of her alarm clock read 12:30 a.m.

"Quinn, your friends are missing," her mother said, her voice now riddled with anxiety, all pretense of calm gone.

Quinn grunted and scooted away, but her mother pulled her back, turning her by the shoulder until Quinn was finally looking at her. Even in the dark, Quinn could see the worry etched into her mother's face. "Quinn, it's important. Annie, Jess and Gina are missing. Do you know where they are?"

"What?" Quinn groaned and noticed her father standing behind her mother, his clean-shaven face every bit as grim as hers.

"Do you know where they are?" her father said, punctuating every word, palpable tension in his voice.

"Who?" Quinn grunted, sleepily rubbing a fist into one eye for dramatic effect.

"Quinn!" Her mother barked. "Pay attention. Annie, Jess, and Gina. Were they headed somewhere after you left Annie's house?"

"I don't know. Why are you asking me?" Quinn replied.

"Because they're gone. They aren't in Annie's house. It's after midnight and Annie's mother can't find them anywhere. Jess's and Gina's parents don't know where they are either. Do you really not know where they went?"

"They're probably running around the neighborhood or something—playing 'Murder in the Dark' or whatever." Quinn yanked the duvet over her head and turned away again.

"They're not in the neighborhood," her mother said. "Their parents have been driving around looking for them. Quinn, if you know something, please tell us. They shouldn't be out in the middle of the night on their own."

"How would I know where they are?" Quinn said, her breath hot on her face, trapped beneath the sheet. "I've been here for hours. They'll turn up. They're not in danger or anything. Their parents are being stupid—just worried for nothing."

"You're sure you don't know?" her father pressed. "They didn't tell you where they might go?"

"No," Quinn moaned. "Now, pleeeaaase—let me go back to sleep."

She sensed her parents hovering by the edge of the bed as if debating whether to push harder, but eventually they left, shutting the door behind them. Quinn remained motionless, pretending to have dozed off, in case one of them checked on her. Sure enough, the door squeaked open five minutes later, only to squeak shut again. Apparently, whichever parent it was believed she had fallen back asleep.

But she wasn't asleep. Still buried beneath the sheet, Quinn's eyes were wide, the th-thump of her heart against her ribcage so loud in her ears that she wouldn't be surprised if her mother could hear it in the hallway. She could feel the tide of stress rising, and fear drove a flash of heat across her skin because she knew what that meant. Stress brought on migraines and the last thing she needed right now was one of those. A feverish nausea broiled in her center, making her stomach turn.

She had told her parents that she didn't know where her friends were. That she had no idea what they were doing. That she was sure they weren't in danger.

But that wasn't true.

As usual, every single word she had uttered was a lie.

2

Thirty-year-old Quinn Bello's hands trembled as she gripped the leather-wrapped steering wheel of her 3 Series BMW with one hand and lifted the other to take a long, last drag on her cigarette. She inhaled deeply, praying for the nicotine to kick in, to soothe...but there was nothing. She crushed the end in the makeshift ashtray of her cupholder. There was no calm to be found in the cigarette, or in the anxiety medication Dr. Bristol had prescribed, or in the alprazolam she had topped it all off with an hour ago to soften the jagged edges.

The cabin of her car seemed to grow smaller by the second, the heat of her own body and electricity of her nerves filling the space to the point of suffocation. The air seemed to be evaporating. Though she sucked in lungfuls, she could not catch her breath. She punched the blue button on the dash to lower the temperature, but the chilly air spilling from the vents did nothing to stave off the sweat that was beading at her brow, then forming tiny rivulets down her hairline. It was a comfortable day in Tampa for November— just seventy-nine degrees—but she would have sworn it was

4

over one hundred degrees in her car even in the shaded garage.

Half an hour ago she had pulled into the parking garage on Twiggs Avenue adjacent to the Hillsborough County Courthouse in downtown Tampa. And there she still sat, paralyzed in the driver's seat, waiting, hoping—striving—to bring herself under control. Tremors rippled through her as her eyes flashed to the briefcase on the black leather seat beside her, then to the dashboard clock.

9:15.

They would call the civil docket at 9:30. Her motion was scheduled to be one of the first.

Pull yourself together, Quinn.

She slapped down the vanity mirror on her sun visor and barely recognized the haggard person in the reflection. Dull, ashen skin had replaced her normally fresh and fair complexion. Bruise-like shadows covered the puffy skin beneath her eyes. They had lost their bright, emerald cast, and now better resembled a drab, army-green. Even her red hair, typically shimmering with golden highlights, was lackluster. She flipped the mirror back up, disgusted.

Tracy Norwich was counting on her. Tracy was the plaintiff in a wrongful death suit against a local cab company for an accident that caused the death of her husband. One of the company's drivers, permitted to continue working despite two DUIs on his record, had struck George Norwich as he crossed the road in broad daylight. Tracy hired Quinn's firm, Cable & Hearn, to represent her in the matter, or more specifically, hired Quinn. She had cried in Quinn's office as Quinn comforted her and promised to do all in her power to make things as right as they could be under the circumstances. The hearing today was on the motion for summary judgment filed by the defendant cab company which, if successful, would end Tracy's two-million-dollar claim for compensatory and punitive damages.

And with all that at stake, Quinn Bello—Attorney at Law, plain-tiff's counselor, champion for tragic victims of unjust offenders —was completely losing it in her own car, with just fifteen minutes to spare.

This case wasn't the only thing riding on the outcome of today's motion. After only four years of practice, Quinn was being considered for a junior partnership at Cable & Hearn. Whether or not she got it depended in large part on today's result. So she had to be *on*. But her body was not cooperating. She could sense the beginning of a migraine pressing on her temples. Chills ran over her skin, triggering a shiver that pulsed through every muscle in her body, shaking her to her core. She gasped once, then let her breath escape in spiky, uneven releases—then gasped again when she saw something move at the edge of her vision in the shadows of the far right corner of the parking deck, about a dozen cars away.

Her head snapped to it.

It wasn't the first time today she had seen shadows where they shouldn't be—flickers of movement in what ought to be empty places.

Someone is following me.

Just an hour before, in the parking garage of her Channel District condominium, she had gotten a creepy vibe from the man who rode the elevator down with her. She didn't recognize him as a resident and she could just *feel* him watching her as she stepped out. Even without looking, her intuition told her he was following her as she walked to her car's assigned spot. Her heartbeat accelerated as his steps drew nearer and nearer, until she finally spun around and screamed at him.

But he hadn't been behind her. In fact, he was actually several car lengths away headed in the opposite direction. Panic mounting, and wondering how in the world she could have gotten it so wrong, Quinn had climbed into her BMW without offering an apology or explanation and peeled past the man, leaving him wide-eyed and open-mouthed.

Remembering the exchange only quickened the pace of her breathing. She closed her eyes and inhaled, trying to rein it in. Then she opened them again, squinting at the spot in the far corner, searching for something, anything, that could have caused the movement she had detected. But there were only vehicles, unmanned, empty.

But something had moved. So what did I see? And where did it go?

Fear swelled but she worked to swallow the panic. To shove it down. To bury it. Because she had to.

She wanted to call her fiancé, Simon, and tell him what had happened. Have him reassure her that everything would be okay and that she was safe. She wanted to hear him say he would leave the hospital right then and come to her, just to check things out, just to make sure she was all right and nothing was amiss.

But there was no point in calling Simon because Quinn knew he wouldn't say any of that. Instead he would tell her she was seeing things. That she was losing it and had better get it together or get some help, or it would kill their relationship. The same things he had been telling her for weeks.

"It's nothing," she hissed, shaking her head as if that would dislodge the dark thoughts from her brain. "There was nothing there. It was just a trick of the light."

So had it been a trick of the light earlier, too, in my own parking garage?

Her heart skipped a beat at the thought—a premature ventricular contraction—the way it did sometimes when her nerves were overwrought. Her hand flew to her chest and she held her breath, waiting to see if there would be another irregular beat. There wasn't, thank goodness, and her heart thumped in time again, the force of it resuming its rhythm feeling like a horse kicking her from the inside.

9:17.

She was going to be late. Another shiver consumed her and she desperately glanced at the glove compartment. There *was* a flask in there. One last hope for calm. For peace. But if anyone smelled it...

She abandoned the notion, snatched up the briefcase and slammed the car door behind her, resolutely jogging toward the elevator. She'd already had one swig this morning. A second would be tempting fate.

Like the BMW's cabin, both the parking garage elevator and the short hallway leading to the back entrance of the court-house seemed stiflingly smaller today, as if they were closing in on her too. She breathed heavily, fighting for her lungs to accept the air, as she swung open the glass door to the court-house and slipped inside.

The heat there was even worse than in the car.

Is the air-conditioning broken? How can it possibly be warmer inside?

The heaviness of the sultry air pushed down on her, threatening to drop her to the floor. She dragged the khaki sleeve of her suit jacket across her forehead, leaving a long sweat stain on the forearm, before flashing her lanyard badge at the security station. A grey-haired deputy motioned her through the roped-off lane for courthouse personnel that bypassed both the walk-through metal detector and the conveyor-belt x-ray machine for her belongings.

"Quinn, you all right?" The question came from behind her after she barreled through, uttered by the same deputy. She swung around, noting the deep furrows in his brow, his eyes crinkled in concern.

"What? Yeah, Henry, I'm fine, I'm just late," she said, and forced a smile, but knew it couldn't have looked genuine. Then her stomach turned again and she was fighting off crippling nausea as well as the draining urge to simply pass out.

"Judge Richter's court?" Henry called after her, but she kept going without offering a response. She knew why he was guessing that she was headed to that particular courtroom. Judge Richter was notorious for calling out attorneys who appeared after the docket had started. Henry was likely assuming that was why she was so frazzled, since she only had five minutes to get inside courtroom nine before the hammer would fall.

Oh, if only that were the reason. If only punctuality was all I had to worry about.

Quinn impatiently jabbed the elevator "up" button even though it was already lit, nearly bending back a nail in the process. More than a dozen others waited with her in the small elevator vestibule for one of the four ancient cars to land on level "P." It smelled of mildew, stale cleaner and faint body odor, and did nothing to help her nerves.

Why is it so hot?

So many people were crowded around—attorneys and clients and victims and family members, all heading upstairs to see justice meted out in its slow, lumbering pace. One lawyer greeted her, then another, speaking her name and saying hello, but she only nodded, unable to vocalize anything in return, afraid one word might push her temperamental stomach over the edge.

The seconds were speeding by. Still no elevator. She glanced at her gold Apple watch.

9:24.

When she looked back up, she saw a shaggy, dark-haired man in jeans, a black T-shirt and grey windbreaker staring at her from where he stood on the far side of the vestibule. There were a dozen people between them, but his gaze seemed trained on her. He glanced away when she caught his eye, something guilty in his expression.

Why is he watching me? Was he what I saw moving in the garage? Was he the shadow in the corner?

But if he was, and he was here now, wouldn't he have had to come through security shortly after her? Wouldn't she have seen him enter? Security was just across from the elevators and in full view from where she stood.

Then again, I've been so distracted, trying not to be sick. It's possible I might not have noticed him going through.

9:27.

There was nothing else for it. Sick or not, she couldn't be late. Tracy Norwich and her promotion depended on it. Giving up on the elevators, she ran for the stairs.

QUINN HURTLED through the double doors to courtroom nine with one minute to spare, nearly tackling a female attorney and her client standing just inside the doorway, conversing quietly.

"Sorry," Quinn mumbled, as she scanned the benches in the gallery for Tracy, a bout of dizziness rocking her.

Tracy Norwich shot up from her seat in the second row, a tsunami of relief visibly rolling over her thin, high-cheekboned face. The thirty-eight-year-old, with her honey-blonde hair and waifish frame, was a direct contrast to Quinn who stood at five-eight, had a mane of thick red hair, and possessed an athletic build she had earned by kayaking every chance she got.

"Quinn!" Tracy called out. Quinn motioned with one hand for her client to lower back down onto the bench as she wove through the packed aisle to join her.

"I didn't think you were going to make it," Tracy squeaked, her face as tight as her voice as Quinn dropped into the seat beside her.

There was a twitchiness in Tracy's manner that evinced her nervousness and Quinn's tardiness likely hadn't helped matters. Though her client looked very put together with her perfectly arranged hair and suitably austere grey dress and black heels, the dark circles beneath her eyes bled through the multiple layers of concealer she had painted over them, evidencing her exhaustion. Those eyes narrowed as she appraised Quinn critically. "What's wrong?"

"What? Nothing. It's fine. I'm here." Quinn could hear the breathiness in her own voice as she pulled her briefcase onto her lap and started fiddling with the latches.

"No," Tracy said. "What's wrong with you? You're sweating —you're practically dripping—and you're—"

"Quinn."

Quinn jumped at the deep voice calling her name from somewhere behind her. Jerking her gaze from Tracy, she spun in her seat, scanning the area at the back of the courtroom. No one seemed to be looking at her.

Who called my name?

"Did you hear that?" Quinn asked, her eyes still trained on the back of the room. "Did someone call me?"

"Quinn, seriously, are you all right?" Tracy asked, tugging on Quinn's arm. "Quinn?"

Quinn rotated forward, her stomach now revolving in nauseating circles. She swallowed hard.

Was the air conditioning broken in here too?

"All rise," the bailiff called, as Judge Laura Richter emerged from her chambers through a door behind the bench and moved to her seat.

Everyone, including Tracy and Quinn, stood in unison— and suddenly the world plummeted. Quinn's hand shot out, grabbing onto Tracy to keep from tipping over as the floor wobbled beneath her. She sucked in a ragged breath as Tracy's fingers firmly clasped Quinn's arm, supporting her weight. As

Quinn struggled to right herself, the bailiff was already striding over. He passed through the swinging gate leading into the gallery, leaning in toward the two women.

"Ms. Bello?" he asked. "You all right? You don't look so good."

"Bailiff, is there a problem there?" Judge Richter called out as she rose to her feet again.

"Quinn, I don't think you're okay," Tracy said, her face flushed and her voice ripe with worry. "Should you be doing this? Should we ask for—"

Whatever else Tracy said, Quinn couldn't hear it. Though the woman's mouth was moving, her voice had evaporated, leaving only the unmistakable sound of the heavy doors at the rear of the courtroom swinging open.

Certain dread filled Quinn as somehow she *knew*, even before she panned toward the rear of the room in what felt like slow motion, and saw him. The shaggy man from downstairs, the one who had been watching her in the elevator vestibule, was headed straight for her. His black, malevolent eyes were locked on her, his shoulders bearing forward as he reached inside his grey windbreaker and whipped out a gun—

"Gun!" Quinn screamed.

The room erupted in shouting and frantic movements as Quinn wrested the deputy's sidearm from his holster, pointed it at the man and fired.

3

Six Months Later

Quinn stepped back from the living room wall, admiring it with a sense of satisfaction, the wet paint roller still in her hand. "Looks good," she said, noting again that the light-cream color had done much to brighten the kitchen and living room spaces. These open, combined areas took up most of the first floor of the three-story beach house overlooking the turquoise waters of the Gulf of Mexico.

The last of the day's sunlight spilled into the space through the floor-length windows and French doors on the beach side of the house that opened to a porch complete with bed swing and rocking chairs. Ready for a break after two straight hours of painting, Quinn set the roller in the tray and headed outside.

The sea air hit her the moment she stepped onto the porch's wooden planks, the salty breeze ruffling her hair as she plopped into the first of the white rockers. She looked beyond the sand dunes and seagrass, roped off for protection, to a lone walker on the beach hugging the water's foamy edge—a good thirty yards from the house even at high tide.

Number Four, Bello Breakers, was the fourth of five nearly identical homes built in a semi-circle on a tract of oceanfront property in the town of Seaglass Cove, Florida. The little unincorporated community lay in the crook of the Big Bend of Florida, just before the state's panhandle coast turned south, becoming the Florida peninsula.

More than a century ago, Seaglass Cove began as a fishing village. Over the last several decades it had transformed into a quiet resort town occupied year-round by locals and seasonally by snowbirds and spring and summer travelers seeking a more relaxed, noncommercial atmosphere. It was surrounded by several national and state parks. Some were entirely inland, with swamps and freshwater springs; others stretched to the coast and included protected beaches, marshlands and even a large coastal dune lake.

Seaglass Cove also boasted one of the few long stretches of white, sugar-sand public beach in the Big Bend area. All that, combined with extensive fishing opportunities, wildlife-oriented parks and a thriving art and culinary community, made the area an appealing alternative to the rowdy, spring-break coastal towns to its west, for those seeking something more laid-back.

Decades before, town leaders had the foresight to enact ordinances precluding the construction of anything other than single-family dwellings along Seaglass Cove's 2000-foot beachfront, avoiding the massive condominium complexes that consumed much of Florida's Panhandle shores. Bello Breakers sat toward the western end of the beach, perched on a moon-shaped, slightly elevated bluff that jutted out toward the Gulf. The development had been built by Quinn's father, Nate Bello, through his realty business, Bello Realty, ten years before. The company owned and managed many properties, including all five homes in Bello Breakers. With the exception of Number Four Bello Breakers, the units were leased to both long- and short-term tenants who paid top dollar for the stunning clapboard residences, each painted a different shade of palest pink, green, yellow and lavender.

Number Four Bello Breakers, painted a soothing light blue, was the house Quinn's mother and father had lived in for the last year, until moving out in early March when they retired to Delray Beach. Quinn took over both the realty business and the house then, and though it wasn't the more modest two-story house she had grown up in on the north side of town, it already felt like home. For the time being, it was hers and she was grateful for it.

Quinn inhaled, long and deep, filling her lungs with the ocean air. She could swear she actually *felt* her blood pressure dropping. Nothing did as much for her peace of mind as this— living right here on the Gulf's edge, with the waves crashing, the sun sparkling on the crystal water by day, the moon dancing on the slippery tide at night. There was something indescribably spiritual and healing about it.

And boy, do I need healing.

A hint of late-day coolness in the air wafted over Quinn and she crossed her arms, warming herself. It was already past seven, and the sun was due to set in about an hour. The sky was turning pink and orange, with faint purple ribbons flaring out across the horizon. A gull squawked and dipped, then soared upward, as Quinn's stomach growled, reminding her that once again, she had worked straight through dinnertime.

As she mentally reviewed what she had in the fridge that she could throw together for dinner—*nothing*—her cell rang, and she pulled it out of her pocket, leaving a thin smear of cream-colored paint on the pocket of her old jeans.

She felt her mouth turn down. Once again, she didn't recognize the number. These unsolicited calls seemed to be coming more often.

Time to re-register on that Do-Not-Call List.

She declined the call as her stomach rumbled a second time. Unless she wanted a bowl of cereal, Pepe's was, like most nights, her best option. But as it was early May, and the busy summer season hadn't started yet, he would close up by 7:30.

Better hustle.

Urgency quickening her steps, Quinn headed back inside, speaking to the electronic *Riki* smart device on the kitchen counter—a foot-high black cylinder with a microphone and speaker—as she passed it.

"Riki, add chicken, steak, and shrimp to the shopping list." The digital assistant, linked to her online accounts and music apps, repeated the additions back to her in its pleasant, simulated human voice. Quinn had to begin stocking her own protein if she ever wanted to cook for herself, instead of dashing off to Pepe's nightly. She passed the clock on the stove which read 7:13, and picked up speed.

If she hurried, she could just make it.

PEPE'S TACO Truck was a permanent fixture of an area of Seaglass Cove known as "The Green" located right on Highway 98—the beach highway that ran parallel to the shoreline for much of the Florida Panhandle. The Green was a square, grassy space, half the size of a football field, dotted with towering long-leaf pines and white wood benches. Its north, east and west sides were bordered by streets lined with unique shops, local restaurants and loft condominiums. The southern side, bordered by Highway 98, sat directly across from the Seaglass Cove Beach parking lot and boardwalk leading to the water.

The streets leading away from The Green wound through

quiet residential areas packed with homes half-occupied by permanent residents, half by rotating snowbirds and vacationers. Many houses incorporated Victorian-esque features, lending a quaint charm to the place furthered by the community's old-fashioned wrought iron street lamps that popped on when dusk fell.

The Green was the hub of Seaglass Cove's activities, and in two weeks it would be hopping late into the night once schools were out and families from all over the Southeast descended. Concerts, barbecues and shrimp boils, Saturday farmers markets, and art strolls would be held throughout the high season. In those coming days, Pepe's Taco Truck—one of four food trucks that would be parked along the edge of The Green all summer—would be serving Oaxaca cheese and Ancho Chile quesadillas, charred tomato salsa burritos, and shrimp nachos right up to ten o'clock at night.

But it wasn't the summer season yet. Pepe's was the only truck on The Green and it would definitely close by seven thirty. So even though The Green was less than a half mile from Bello Breakers and Quinn could have easily walked there, tonight she drove, zooming up in her white pickup and swinging into one of the gravel parking spaces along the highway. She darted across the blacktop and dashed to the sliding window of the bright red truck with habanero peppers painted on the side to see the proprietor busy inside cleaning the grill.

"Hey, Miguel," Quinn called into the window, a bit breathless. "Got time for one more?"

"Hey, Quinn," he said, turning away from the grill to face her, a wide smile breaking out on his face, his black hair falling to either side of his forehead. He dropped the cloth he was using and stepped to the window. "How's it going?"

"Good. Finished painting today."

"Nice." Miguel was one of the few people Quinn had connected with since moving back. Though plenty of people knew her and of her in Seaglass Cove, she hadn't gone out of her way to rekindle any of those old relationships. After what happened in Tampa, and her preexisting hometown reputation in Seaglass Cove, the last thing she wanted was to deal with any of the fallout from her checkered past.

Come to think of it, Miguel is one of the few people I interact with at all.

Her lack of social engagement was partly due to the incessant amount of work involved in running the realty company. But mostly her reclusiveness was intentional. She had hurt enough people. She wasn't ready to risk hurting any more. She could count on one hand the people she regularly spoke to in town: Miguel, Terri Colbert—the woman who managed the realty office—Lena and others at the Hope Community Center where Quinn volunteered, a few at Hope Community Church, and—

"We have skirt steak left," Miguel said, cutting off Quinn's internal list-making just as one final name came to mind—one that sparked a hint of heat at her collar.

"Perfect," she said, digging some cash from her pocket while Miguel prepared her street tacos, her stomach growling again as the scent of tomato, chilies and cheese wafted through the window.

This casual friendship with Miguel wasn't something she had sought out. It was simply a side product of the fact that cooking wasn't her thing and planning menus, even less. It was just easier to hop over and grab something from Miguel most nights. Their chatting started when Quinn first stopped by and upon seeing the name "Miguel" on his name tag, asked where the name of the truck—"Pepe"—came from. Turned out, that was Miguel's grandfather's nickname. Quinn loved that. All of her grandparents had passed on and she missed them terribly. Family had always been hugely important to her. But now her clan consisted solely of her, her mom and dad, and a few scattered cousins she never heard from anymore.

She watched as Miguel filled a cup with the liquid gold cheese dip she loved, and realized wistfully she would have to start incorporating more exercise into her routine if chips and queso were going to be a staple of her diet. Most weeks, she only managed to get the kayak in the water once, which wasn't nearly enough. She missed it greatly, and not just because it would keep the inevitable fluffiness around her middle at bay. She needed it for her emotional well-being, and resolved right then and there to find a way to make room for more paddle time.

On the short drive home, the zesty aroma of cilantro and chiles filled her pickup, leaving her mouth watering at the thought of the corn tacos filled with skirt steak, cheese and salsa, and Miguel's signature black beans and rice. In half a minute she was back at Bello Breakers, punching in the four-digit security code that opened the white picket gate at the entrance. The community wasn't fenced in, but the gate prevented random drivers from using Bello Breakers Circle and their driveways as an overflow parking lot for the beach or The Green, on days when the public spots were all taken.

She felt a smile crease her face as she drove around the one-way concrete-paver roundabout, with its zoysia grass center and the illuminated stone swordfish fountain gurgling away. Darkness had fallen now, and lights shone from the windows of all five of the Bello Breakers houses. They stood like guards on the semi-circle knoll, facing outward, keeping watch over the sea, set in a staggered fashion that afforded each of them privacy on their porches as well as the best views of the water possible in both directions. Though the houses were all three stories high, the lots themselves were quite narrow, leaving just enough room for a thin slice of yard between them.

Mrs. Garber, the current lessee of Number Two—the pink

house—happened to be in her driveway and waved at Quinn as she passed. The Garbers were a lovely sixty-something couple wrapping up a three-week stay the next day. Quinn made a mental note to stop by in the morning to say goodbye, then pulled into her own drive, which was really nothing more than a two-car-wide parking space at the rear of the house. Grasping her takeout, she walked under the small white wooden portico over the back door, unlocked it and slipped inside. She stopped long enough to kick off her running shoes, sending them rolling across the tan ceramic tile toward the reclaimed wood bench in the entryway, then kept going into the kitchen, intent on grabbing a bottle of blackberry-infused water before heading out to the porch to eat. But just steps from the stainless steel fridge, she froze.

Twelve feet in front of her, sprawled on the floor beside the granite bar that separated the kitchen from the living room, lay a man clad in khakis and a light-green, long-sleeved button-down shirt. He was unnaturally still, his right arm stretched out as if reaching for something. The other arm was buried beneath his torso. His head, turned in Quinn's direction, revealed glassy light-brown eyes that stared at the wall with no hint of life in them whatsoever.

For a few heartbeats, Quinn seized, her brain working to catch up with the reality in front of her. All warmth drained from her body, replaced by a horrifying chill reaching into every cell. A piercing scream erupted from her lips and she spun, running for the door.

4

Quinn tore from the back of her house, flinging the door open wildly. Her heart pounded against her ribs as she ran past her pickup, clipping it with her right side, ripping the takeout container from her hands so that tacos, rice and beans spilled out, splattering on the driveway. She charged straight for the back door of Number Three—the lavender house to the left—crossing the short twenty-five-foot distance in seconds. She banged violently on its white back door—identical to hers—her fists soon stinging from the force of her pounding. When five seconds passed and no one answered, Quinn violently punched the doorbell in rapid succession.

Still nothing. Her eyes shot to her own back door, expecting —what? The man to walk out?

Those eyes...those vacant brown eyes. The man was gone. Dead.

So what was she watching her door for?

His killer.

Another spasm of fear gripped Quinn as she continued banging and squinted through the textured glass panes in the top of the door. There were lights on in the house, but no sign of movement. Abandoning the attempt, she raced toward Number Two, where she *knew* Mrs. Garber was home. At the door, she lifted her hand to pound again—when mental lightning struck. Feeling sick for not thinking of it sooner, she grabbed her cell from her pocket and entered 9-1-1 with the thumb of one hand while alternately pounding on the door and jabbing the bell with her other hand.

Light and shadow shifted across the panes in the top of the door. At the same time Quinn pressed the phone's dial icon, the door swung open revealing a confused Mrs. Garber, her eyebrows pressing high into her wrinkled forehead as the 9-1-1 operator answered.

THE LIGHTS from three Wilson County Sheriff's Department cruisers flashed red and blue against the homes in Bello Breakers, like bizarre disco projections on the pastel structures, creating a dizzying rainbow effect. They had arrived nearly simultaneously, parking behind Number Four's driveway, blocking in Quinn's pickup. Quinn and the Garbers stepped out from the safety of Number Two to watch from their portico as the deputies exited their vehicles, weapons drawn, and entered Number Four. By this time the residents of Numbers One and Five had also stepped out to see what was happening. Number Three was still AWOL.

The deputies were only inside Quinn's house for a few minutes before one emerged from the back door, standing tall in his dark-grey uniform with a Wilson County gold-embroidered emblem affixed high on both sleeves. Dread pricked Quinn's gut as she recognized him immediately. Shane Cody was a fellow graduate of Wilson County High School, someone she hadn't seen in more than ten years, and as far as she knew, still couldn't stand the sight of her. On top of everything else, this was the last thing she needed.

"Quinn? Quinn Bello?" he shouted in her direction, angling his head.

"Yeah," she answered, hearing the note of trepidation in her voice. Another deputy exited her house, walked behind Shane and made his way to the center of the roundabout, scanning and turning as he went, his weapon still at the ready.

Shane crooked a finger, motioning at her. "Come on over, Quinn," he called out.

"You sure? Whoever did that to him isn't still in there?"

He nodded. "The house is clear. We're still checking outside, but I need you to come in with me, please. Okay?"

Quinn started toward him, the Garbers following closely behind, when Shane threw up a hand. "Just Ms. Bello, please, folks," he cautioned, and they stopped where they stood as Quinn went on alone.

As she drew closer, she got a better look at her old classmate. Other than some crinkling around his eyes and skin weathered from many summer tans, Shane Cody looked just as Quinn remembered—blue eyes, curly blonde hair and freckles across the bridge of his nose. She also thought she could see the disdain she remembered simmering behind his stare.

"You all right?" he asked.

She nodded, angry with herself that she had forgotten he was a sheriff's deputy. Her mother had mentioned it once in passing, but tonight she had been so freaked out, it hadn't occurred to her that he might show up. So now, as if this event wasn't horrible enough, he was here, and this whole thing had become even more surreal.

"We've cleared the house." He nodded toward the other deputy, now working his way toward Number Five. "We're checking paths between the houses and the beach, but there's no sign of an intruder."

"And the man on the floor? Who is he?"

He tilted his head toward the house. "Let's go inside. Have a chat."

As an attorney, Quinn had been around law enforcement personnel enough to know that they saw disturbing situations on a regular basis, numbing them to the point that they could take something like finding a corpse on the floor in stride. However, something about Shane's unruffled demeanor was so completely unaffected—even more so than she would have expected—that it concerned her. From his reaction, you would have thought she reported someone rolled her house, not that she came home to find a dead man on her floor.

Shane held the back door open, allowing her to pass. She only had to go a few feet into the entryway to know exactly what he wanted to chat about and why he was so impassive.

The spot on the floor where the corpse had lain just fifteen minutes earlier was empty.

DEPUTY CODY SAT beside Quinn on the creamy velvet couch in her living room. He was rigid and all business, while in contrast, she had shrunk into the pillows, a cotton knit throw gathered around her as she clutched a bottle of water. He had been thoughtful enough to retrieve it from the fridge for her, and the icy cold was like an anchor.

"Describe it again," he said, leaning forward, his arms propped on his knees.

"I've told you everything, Shane," Quinn said, unable to keep the note of exasperation out of her voice. "Twice." She knew he was just trying to get the story straight, but repeating it wasn't going to change anything. "I don't want to go through it again. I want to know *where the body went.*"

"I know, Quinn. And I don't have an answer for you. At least not one you're going to want to hear."

Her skin tingled in warning. "What's that supposed to mean?"

He rolled his lips inward before speaking, then released them. "Have you considered—I mean, given that there just isn't any sign of a corpse—that maybe you didn't see exactly what you thought you saw?"

"I'm sorry," she said, pivoting toward him, her back straightening. "There was a dead guy on my floor, Shane. Not much room for misinterpretation."

"Well, except, there is no dead guy on your floor."

She sucked in a breath. "What exactly are you suggesting?"

"Quinn, we've checked your entire house several times. No one is here who shouldn't be—living or dead. I'm suggesting that maybe—just humor me—maybe it wasn't a dead person on your floor. I'm not saying someone wasn't here, I'm just saying that maybe they just got up and walked away."

Quinn ran a hand over her face. She should have expected this. Of course, they wouldn't believe her. Of course, *he* wouldn't believe her. "Shane, please. I know dead when I see it."

"But there's no one here, Quinn—"

"So you're saying he, what...broke in, then somehow knocked himself out cold, then woke up while I ran off for help and just waltzed out of here?"

Shane sighed and his arm twitched, as if he was going to reach out, possibly touch her arm in a gesture of understanding. Maybe that was something he did with other victims he interviewed. But whatever his initial instinct, his arm stilled, remaining where it was. And that was fine with her. She wouldn't have wanted him to do it anyway. When it came to her, the gesture would have been forced and fake and, therefore, completely pointless.

"Quinn, I'm not trying to be difficult. Honestly. I'm just trying to make sense of what you're telling me, given that there isn't a body here."

He really did sound like he meant it. And, if she looked at it from his perspective, she could see where he was coming from.

But if I were anyone else, would he be so reluctant to take my story at face value?

She stared at him, trying to figure out how to get through to him, knowing she wouldn't be able to. She also couldn't help but think of all the things she should be saying to Shane Cody now that she was seeing him for the first time after so long. But she said none of them, and in fact, they both seemed to be pretending they didn't need saying. Because at this moment, he was Deputy Shane Cody, random responder to a call about a murdered person who had vanished into thin air, not Shane Cody, former friend of Quinn Bello and close cousin of Annie Cody.

He sniffed, interrupting her thoughts. "Has anything been taken?"

Had anything been taken? She cast around, but nothing jumped out at her. "I've barely been home. I don't know. I'll have to look."

"Okay, so do that. Look things over, see if anything's missing and let us know. Because right now, my best guess is this was a robbery gone bad, probably involving two people who got into it and you just stumbled onto the aftermath."

"Do most robbers wear green button-downs and khakis?" She knew it was a valid point. That wasn't exactly the uniform of your standard house burglar. He had to know it too.

Even so, he eyed her warily, a hint of irritation in the gesture, and pinched his lips together again before speaking. "Just check for anything that's missing, okay?"

Her insides prickled, as she realized he was dismissing the clothing issue. Her annoyance must have shown on her face, because Shane fidgeted, shifting his weight. "Look, Quinn, I hear you. I do. But whatever happened, I don't think someone died here tonight."

The prickling grew sharper, her indignance mounting. She knew what she had seen. The fact that the body wasn't there didn't change that. "What if someone carted him off? What if there *were* two people and whoever did that to him was still here when I got home, then dragged him off when I left?"

"Someone would have noticed a person carrying off a body. They would have reported it."

"Who? We're pretty isolated right here. He could have just slipped down the walkway or even over the dunes. Maybe there's tracks—"

"We'll check, Quinn. I promise. But footprints in the sand aren't going to tell us anything. They could've been put there at any time. I'm sorry, but without more to go on, I think we have to label this a break-in."

She sighed and looked beyond him, out through the glass porch doors. The beach was pitch-black now. There was hardly any moon, just a sliver, the thinnest of C's. She could hear the roar of the ocean, but couldn't see the water at all. The darkness only made her feel more lost. Nothing was making sense.

"Are you going to be all right by yourself here tonight? Can we call someone for you?" Her eyes flicked back to him. So that was it. He wasn't going to believe her. She sighed and the fight went out of her. Faced with these circumstances and her history —their history—she might have drawn the same conclusions he had.

"I'll be fine," she said. "I've got an alarm system."

"Doesn't do you any good if you don't use it."

He was right. She hadn't set it before leaving. She hadn't set the thing in probably a month. "Well, I'll start," she said. It was just a pain to deal with, especially when so often she was just running out for a second, like whenever she headed down to Pepe's. But now she would have to change that.

He stood, but she didn't move. "I'll let you know if we find anything else," he told her, holding out a business card. "We'll need an inventory of anything taken. You can just email it to me if you want."

His "if you want" sounded less than enthusiastic.

Quinn took the card and nodded weakly. "Sure."

Shane clasped his hands in front of him and suddenly seemed less official, his posture curving a bit as he rocked from foot to foot. "I, uh, heard you were back."

Oh. So we're going to do this now.

"Little over five months," she replied. She had returned to Seaglass Cove in December for the holidays and while waiting for the resolution of the mess in Tampa.

"No, I meant, back from rehab."

His words pierced her. Leave it to him to not only bring up that she had left town for a month in January for rehab, but to use it like a weapon to chip away at her.

What were you expecting from him, Quinn? Grace?

"Oh, that," she offered, trying to inject a note of indifference into her tone. "Well, in that case, it'd be three months now."

"Sorry," he said, but the pointedness of his gaze suggested that he wasn't sorry at all. "I just...know that the transition can be hard. I hope you're doing okay. That it's still...going well."

Ah, there it is, Quinn thought, finally making the connection. *He wants to be sure there isn't another explanation for why I saw a body on the floor that isn't there.*

She inhaled deeply and forced a smile. "It's going great, actually," she said, and she meant it. Because it was.

"Good. That's really good," he replied. But his eyes were just slits as his head cocked to one side, starkly appraising her, and she knew that no matter what came out of his mouth, he wasn't automatically taking her answer for the truth.

"Thanks, Shane." *Thanks for making me feel even worse.*

"I was surprised to hear you were taking over the realty business for your dad—I mean, you being an attorney and everything. Surprising career change."

Does he really not know what happened in Tampa? Is that possible, given the rumor mill in this town? Or did he ask because he does know and wants to push me, wants to hear me say the words?

Either way, she wasn't going there.

"Well, it's good to see you," she said, rising to match him, hoping that this would be enough to get him out the door.

But instead he just stood there, eyeing her as if trying to unscramble a code, and her heart began thumping harder. *Is he waiting for me to ask? Waiting for me to broach the subject hanging in the air between us?*

If so, he was wasting his time. She had no desire to bring up the past, and especially not *that*. Because while asking would have been polite—would have shown she still felt responsible and appropriately remorseful—it would have driven her to even lower depths. So considering that he already thought so little of her, she figured a bit of impoliteness wouldn't make much difference and kept her mouth shut.

After a few more seconds of awkward silence, he reminded her once more to make a list of anything that was missing, and then finally, thankfully, left. She immediately locked up behind him, then—even though the deputies already had—checked the windows and doors to make sure they were locked too as she heard the patrol cars start up, then pull away.

For the next twenty minutes she paced through every room, looking for anything that might be missing. But as far as she could tell everything was in its place. The obvious items—her laptop, checkbooks, even the cash she kept in the desk drawer in her office—were all present and accounted for. She headed upstairs to the third floor, which consisted of two spartan guest rooms, a bathroom and a sitting room, all of which appeared untouched. Finally she headed back down to the second floor which held the master suite—her bedroom—and two other bedrooms that shared a Jack-and-Jill bath. Everything was exactly as it should be. Even her jewelry box was intact, an undisturbed, fine layer of dust on top.

This was no robbery, she thought as she closed the jewelry box. But doubt quickly surfaced. *Or could Shane be right? Was it a robbery, but something went wrong before they could take anything?*

She collapsed onto her king-sized bed, frazzled, frustrated, and a little bit scared. Lying there, trying to process it all, the exhaustion she had been fighting for the last couple of hours overtook her. With her clothes still on she crawled beneath the waffle-weave blanket and crisp white duvet, her stomach grumbling noisily, reminding her that she had never eaten. She ignored it. At this point, she was too tired to do anything but sleep.

But it was a long time before she drifted off. Every time Quinn closed her eyes, the image of the corpse's light-brown ones staring blankly out at the world flickered on the back of her lids, like an old-fashioned, silent horror movie. She could almost hear the whirring and clicking of an ancient projector as the scene played on and on, scored by the incessant questions hammering her brain.

Why my house?
Was I targeted or was it random?
Who was he? And who killed him?
How did they get in and how did the killer leave?
And is he coming back?

Heat simmered on her skin, her frustration mounting as it all rattled around her head. Because no matter how impossible it seemed and no matter what Shane Cody said, she knew to her core that two hours ago a very, *very* dead man had lain on her floor—a man who had broken in for reasons unknown—then vanished without a trace.

So many questions. Absolutely no answers.

And from the looks of things, not a soul was going to believe her.

5

Quinn woke Saturday morning almost as exhausted as she had been when she crawled in bed. Sleep hadn't come until nearly midnight and even then it was broken with nightmares of dead bodies walking in and out of her house. For a while she lay there, sun streaming in through the sheers—she had forgotten to pull the blackout curtains—listening to the water sloshing on the shore and one particularly song-filled sparrow that had landed somewhere on the balcony. Her sleep-deprived mind quickly busied itself replaying the night's events, and in addition to all the other emotions wracking her, Quinn found herself feeling one she hadn't felt last night.

Sadness.

Shane wasn't the first person she had run into from her former life in Seaglass Cove. But he *was* the first one who had been intimately connected to everything that had made her want to leave the town in the first place. It wasn't as if she didn't know something like that would happen eventually. But until last night, she had somehow, blissfully, avoided it. Now with Shane involved in the investigation of last night's events, she would have to see him again. The thought made her stomach drop.

Around seven fifteen, accepting she couldn't put the day off any longer, she threw her legs over the edge of the bed and resolved to face it. If this had been a Sunday, she could have crawled back under the covers until it was time to get ready to leave for church, or if Monday, she could have stayed there pretending none of it had happened since that was her day off. But in her business, Tuesday through Saturday was the standard work week, and with lots of renters typically checking in and out on Saturday, she had plenty lined up to do and needed to get at it.

Terri, the office manager, would be at the office by eight thirty, ready to go. If Quinn buckled down, she might finish up by early afternoon and be able to squeeze in some paddling. She asked *Riki* for the weather report, who replied it was supposed to be a gorgeous day—sunny and 81 degrees. Perfect for some time on the water. Quinn's spirit buoyed at the thought of climbing in her kayak and gliding along in the cool waters overhung by the cypress trees in Cove Springs National Park, just her and nature. She could use a little of that right now.

Determined to make it happen, she bypassed her normal routine, which most days involved scrambling an egg and making her own Peet's Medium Roast from her French press, adding a splash of milk and two cubes of sugar, then savoring both on the back porch while reading the day's entry from her devotional book. The passages always seemed to settle her. Center her for the day ahead. But today called for getting out there as quickly as possible, so instead she showered and pulled on cropped navy pants, a white short-sleeved tunic top and light-grey jacket. After applying minimal makeup and gathering her red tresses into a loose, low ponytail, she grabbed her keys and scooted out the door.

She promised herself she would read the devotional passage later using an app on her phone while skimming along the water, with nothing to distract her. The kayak was such a spiritual place for her anyway, and a perfect place to soak in God's word. It wouldn't hurt to hold off for a few hours.

The coffee, however, couldn't wait.

THE LITTLE RED Shed was a half mile east of The Green, also right on Highway 98. Previously, it actually *had* been a shed of sorts, the main building of a landscaping nursery that went out of business. The siding of the large, one-story structure was painted barn-red, with clean white trim accents, and expansive windows. It sat at the back of a gravel lot surrounded by scrub oaks, longleaf pines and several magnolias. Pebbled paths meandered in multiple directions from the lot, winding through the wide variety of plantings around the sides and back of the building, including palmettos, wildflowers, benches and fountains, creating a garden almost park-like in its serenity.

Quinn had been briefly delayed when she stopped at Bello Breakers Number Two to say goodbye to the Garbers and assure them she was fine. Now, at a little after eight, several cars were already in The Shed's lot, but Quinn was able to park in one of the front spaces. She hopped out, the fragrant scent of something flowery greeting her as gravel crunched beneath her steps. She pushed open the single door on the side of the building that served as the primary entrance and a cowbell suspended over it clanked noisily.

Immediately to her left was an L-shaped reclaimed-wood counter with rattan stools stretched down its length. Shiny coffee and espresso machines lined the back counter. On the wall above that was an enormous blackboard with multi-colored chalk script detailing the menu, featuring breakfast and lunch fare tweaked with local touches. To her right was a sitting area filled with overstuffed chairs and rustic tables—many already occupied—and bookshelves lining the walls with a free-to-borrow library. The remainder of the huge interior of the old nursery was divided into sections dedicated to a myriad of other activities, including a stage, art studio and game and craft area. It was essentially Seaglass Cove's version of a local pub, and though it had only been around for six months, had quickly become a favorite hangout.

It also had the best coffee in town, which was what was on Quinn's mind when she waltzed up to the counter, her fuzzy head begging for a thousand cc's of caffeine, stat. Waiting for her was the person she had been thinking of the night before at Pepe's Taco Truck, when Miguel had interrupted her mental inventory of people she regularly interacted with in Seaglass Cove.

Ian Wolfe.

Ian owned The Little Red Shed and, as far as Quinn knew, worked there every minute it was open because she had never been there once when he wasn't. And since Quinn craved a good cup of coffee pretty regularly, and wasn't opposed to a blackberry muffin with homemade cream filling or avocado toast made with freshly baked Challah either, she had fallen into the habit of stopping in at least every other day. Which was how Ian had made the shortlist of people she saw routinely.

"Hey, Quinn," Ian said, his smile stretching into his deep-set dark eyes. The six-foot-plus, early thirty-something had heather brown hair, cut closely on the sides, but longer on top, creating thick, wiry waves with tips that curled, a random end sticking out here and there. Narrow sideburns reached to the midpoint of his ear, where lean cheekbones drew to a refined nose that—

Stop gawking, Quinn. Say something.

35

"Hi, Ian," she replied, plopping her purse down on the counter. "What's good today?"

The aroma of roasted coffee and baking bread mixed pleasantly with the slight, inviting mustiness of the used books on the shelves in the sitting area, and the soothing scent of lavender emanating from pots on the windowsill next to the counter.

"The special is orange biscuits with honey, and a poached egg on the side with bacon."

"Sold," she said, slapping the counter with one hand, then bringing it up to stifle a yawn.

Ian let a small, amused snort escape. "I'm guessing you're needing a jolt today? Vanilla latte, sprinkle of cinnamon?"

"You're a mind reader."

He smiled wryly. "Nah. You're just a bit predictable when it comes to your coffee."

"Guess I'll have to work on that," Quinn quipped as Ian scribbled on an order pad, then pushed the slip of paper onto the ledge of a large window behind him that opened into the kitchen, where the cook snatched it up.

As Ian started on her latte, Quinn rolled her head, trying to fend off the ache she was already beginning to feel at the base of her skull. It was apparently going to be a long day. Silently she prayed this wasn't going to trigger one of her migraines.

"You all right?" Ian asked, his back still to her as he fiddled with the espresso machine currently dispensing a steaming stream of liquid.

She stopped mid-head roll and eyed the back of him quizzically. "Um, yeah. Do I not look it?"

"No, it's just...well, the yawning. And," he turned around, nodding his head at her, "your jacket's inside out."

Heat flashed across the back of her neck as she looked down and saw the seams of her jacket. "Good grief," she moaned, wriggling out of it and twisting it right side out before sliding her arms back in. "I'm not running on all cylinders. I had a long night."

Behind Quinn a chair scraped hard against the wood floor. She turned to see Meghan Carne, an ebony-haired woman a little younger than Quinn, dressed in a sundress and sandals, sashaying up to the counter. She squeezed in between a couple of bar stools a few spaces down from Quinn and leaned her forearms on the countertop.

"Hi, Quinn," Meghan said, sparing Quinn a quick glance before zeroing in on Ian.

"Hey Meghan," she replied, but the woman wasn't cued in to her any longer.

"Ian," Meghan started, "the coffee was great as always." Her voice was low, almost husky, in sharp contrast to her dainty features and pixie nose.

"Glad to hear it, Meghan."

Was it Quinn's imagination, or had Ian's voice dropped a step or two? The smile he offered Meghan was barely more than a crook at one corner of his mouth, but it was striking, something Meghan apparently thought too, based on the grin she flashed in return. Looking at Ian from beneath her long lashes, Meghan wiggled her red nails as she stepped toward the door.

In the base of her gut, Quinn's nerves tingled caustically.

"See you later?" Meghan asked.

"I'll be here," Ian replied as Meghan stepped through the doorway, her dress rippling in the breeze outside.

Quinn had seen Meghan in The Little Red Shed several times, though usually in the afternoon, and even had a conversation with her once about a suspense novel Quinn was reading while curled up in one of the overstuffed chairs. She didn't learn much about the woman during their short exchange, except that Meghan managed The Lighthouse, one of the finer restaurants in town, and usually wasn't even up until well after noon.

"She's in early," Quinn noted, as Ian turned back to finish her latte.

"It's her day off," he said.

Quinn's heart dropped an inch. Even before today, something about the interactions she had previously witnessed between Meghan and Ian suggested they might be involved, or at least headed in that direction. After this little display, and his thorough knowledge of her schedule, it seemed even more likely.

Oh well, she thought, and then nearly kicked herself for it. *What do you mean, "oh well"? It wasn't as if you were going to do anything about it.*

And that was the truth. The last thing she needed was a romantic complication just as she was re-establishing herself in Seaglass Cove. Besides, she was still healing from the insane events in Tampa. *And*, her engagement to Simon had ended only six months ago, the proverbial grass-barely-grown-over-the-relationship's-grave situation. Finally, and most importantly, she didn't want to hurt anyone else and that was all she ever seemed to do. There was loneliness in that kind of self-imposed isolation, but there was safety in it too. Especially for others.

Ian pushed the latte toward her, a foamy concoction in a wide-brimmed cup, the kind you could wrap both hands around. "The food'll be up in a second," he told her.

"Thanks," she said, and slid onto a barstool. She could have gotten the food to-go, and right about now, was halfway wishing she had. But it would be easier to gobble it down here, rather than trying to juggle eating a poached egg in the car.

Ian stood before her, wiping his hands on a bar towel that he slung over his shoulder. "So, late night? Big date or something?" She looked up from the design of a whale he had traced through the latte's foam—which even included a fountain escaping the whale's blowhole in curly-cues drawn in the steamed milk—to find him grinning at her.

"Impressive," she said, tilting her head at the coffee. She took a sip and the robust flavor hit her as if she had stuck her finger in a socket. She swallowed and sighed. "Um, no. No big date. Not unless you consider your house getting broken into, a date."

His engaging grin became a thin, straight line, his eyebrows drawing together in a concerned "V." "Your house was broken into?" He leaned forward, closing the distance between them to a mere foot or so. "What happened? Are you all right?"

Am I all right? she asked herself, taking stock. *No, I am not all right. And actually it wasn't simply a break-in. It was a murder. With a corpse left behind on my kitchen floor.*

But she wasn't going to tell him any of that. What was the point of sharing all the gory details? She didn't need another person thinking she was seeing things.

"Yeah, I'm fine," she said.

"What did they take?"

Good question. "Nothing as far as I can tell."

His nose wrinkled. "Burglars who don't burgle? That doesn't make much sense."

Exactly, she thought.

"What did the police say?" he pressed.

"The sheriff's deputy said they must've gotten spooked before they were able to make off with anything."

"And?"

"And that's it."

The cook rang the bell at the kitchen window as he slid a plate onto its ledge. Ian stepped away just long enough to bring it back to Quinn. It smelled heavenly. She pulled off a chunk of biscuit and savored it.

"So, you're really okay?" he asked as she cut into the

poached egg and golden yolk ran out. There was a palpable note of worry in his voice that went beyond mere interest and it made her look up.

His eyes were full of genuine concern. She offered him a smile and his expression eased. "Yes, I'm really okay. Just tired from staying up to check everything over."

The cowbell over the door clanked again as more patrons entered. "Is anybody staying with you?" he asked.

"No, but it's okay, really. If it was a random burglar then there isn't much to worry about. At least the deputies weren't too worried."

"Don't you have an alarm?"

Her face wrinkled sheepishly, the fork halfway to her mouth. "I haven't been using it."

"Well, start then." There was a distinct soberness in his tone as he leaned toward her. He wore an untucked, unbuttoned plaid shirt over a form-fitting white T-shirt, his sleeves rolled up to reveal lean, muscled forearms. The scent of something woodsy drifted across the counter.

"Um, well, yeah," Quinn mumbled, unexpectedly finding herself unnerved by his proximity. "That's the plan."

"Good."

Another couple of people came in, causing a line to form at the register. Quinn's eyebrows rose as she inclined her head toward the waiting customers. "Don't you think you better…"

"Yeah, right," he said, shaking his head slightly. "I'm glad you're okay, though. And be careful?"

She nodded, warmed by his sincerity, and gave him a quick, light-hearted two-fingered salute. "Will do."

6

While Ian took the other customers' orders, he kept one eye on Quinn, watching through the window as she got in her pickup, then drove away. But as he continued describing the specials and ringing people up, instead of dissipating, the current of worry that had begun coursing through him at Quinn's mention of a break-in continued to set him on edge.

His reaction surprised him. It wasn't as if he knew her well. Yes, she came in fairly often, and, yes, they always chatted. But it didn't go any further than that. He knew she was the manager of Bello Realty, had started coming in a little over two months ago, and pretty much kept to herself. Other than speaking to him, and the occasional pleasantries he had witnessed her exchange with other customers, he had never known her to have a meaningful conversation with anyone. He also knew she had killer green eyes and thick red hair that cascaded to just below her shoulders whenever she wore it down.

But that was pretty much it. He hadn't made an effort to learn more because, as with nearly all his customers—as with nearly everyone he had met since arriving in Seaglass Cove—

he maintained an intentional, acceptable distance, walking a fine line between being engaging but private. Keeping everything on a safe, superficial level.

So why was she still on his mind?

He was creating a frond pattern on a latte by pouring the steamed milk in just the right way, watching the image emerge as he zig-zagged the little silver pitcher back and forth, when the answer occurred to him.

Because she didn't just seem tired today. She seemed a little bit beaten down.

It wasn't anything he could point to, really. A shadow behind her eyes, maybe? Had there been a hint of defeat in her voice when she was talking about the break-in that he had subconsciously registered? Or maybe it was just a vibe he had picked up on.

Whatever it was, his preoccupation with Quinn Bello after her visit this morning suddenly made sense, because being a little bit beaten down was something he could relate to. Being a little bit beaten down—or in his case, a lot—was something with which he was altogether too familiar.

7

Maybe it was the jolt of caffeine. Ian did make a pretty stout cup of joe. Or maybe it was the fact that she was coming out of her late night stupor and didn't like the idea that she was being brushed off by Shane. Whatever it was, a bout of righteous indignation kicked in a few minutes after she pulled out of The Shed's parking lot, prompting Quinn to make a detour to the Wilson County Sheriff's Department.

The main office of the sheriff's department was a squat brick building on the block behind the Wilson County Courthouse, about four miles inland from Seaglass Cove's beach. This area resembled the quintessential small southern town, replete with a white historic courthouse at the center of a square boasting large, ancient oaks.

Quinn marched through the door of the sheriff's department into a waiting room lined with hard plastic chairs that discouraged anyone from actually waiting in them. She recognized the clerk behind the welcome counter immediately. Maryanne Rowley was a lifelong resident of Seaglass Cove and had known Quinn since she was in elementary school. Which meant she knew all the dirt.

Great.

As Quinn's gaze drifted over the woman's badly-dyed brunette hair, curled and sprayed into a poofy shell, to her red-framed, cat-eye glasses, she saw the flash of recognition in Maryanne's eyes. Dread knotted in Quinn's stomach.

"Well, Quinn Bello! I can't believe it! How are you, honey? How're your mom and dad doing?"

She sounded sincere, and there was even an element of kindness in her tone. That was the thing about it all. The people who had known her back when it happened weren't mean to her. She wasn't treated poorly or ostracized. No one egged her house or called her names or gave her a hard time. From all appearances, the town had forgiven her ages ago.

But like most small towns, this one had a long memory. A long memory that, combined with the news that had undoubt-edly spread about Tampa, perpetuated the whispers behind her back, the not-so-surreptitious stares, and—as last night had demonstrated—a lingering lack of credibility. Yes, the town may have forgiven her. But forgetting wasn't even on the table.

"Hi, Maryanne. I'm good. Mom and Dad are fine."

"You sure you're okay, hon? I heard about the *break-in* last night." She wrapped her tongue bitingly around "break-in" and Quinn knew immediately that Shane must have already told everyone in the department about his doubts. A stifled cough sounded from somewhere in the room behind the counter, and Quinn's gaze shot to two deputies standing together on the far side of the room, staring at her and mouthing something she couldn't hear. She didn't have to be a lip-reader to guess the topic of their discussion.

"I'm here to see Shane—Deputy Cody—about that. Is he in?" Quinn asked.

"No, hon. Sorry. He's second shift. Doesn't come on until three."

"Oh, right." *Of course he wouldn't be in yet. He was working last night.*

"I can give him a message, though," Maryanne offered helpfully.

"Would you tell him I stopped by? I wanted to run through things with him. He asked for a list of anything that was missing—"

"You could just email that," Maryanne interrupted.

"Yeah, I know, but I was hoping to talk to him in person. And there isn't a list, because there isn't anything missing as far as I can tell."

"Oh. Well, that's good," Maryanne said, her words coated in a syrupy drawl thicker than what the local Griddle House served on its pancakes.

Quinn sighed. If Shane had shared his doubts about her story, it meant that these three, and probably everybody else in the department, had one more reason to whisper. One more reason to be skeptical of her in general. Ever since she was a kid she had been branded a liar in this town—or at the very least, unreliable—and now, after Tampa and last night...

It seemed no matter how hard she tried to shake the label, no matter what good she tried to do, life kept throwing her past sins back in her face. This bitter reality twisted her insides, and the energy boost she'd enjoyed after Ian's coffee seemed to drain away.

Maybe there was no shaking it. Maybe the cold, hard truth was that the person they all thought she was, was the only person they were ever going to see.

ONCE BACK IN the sheriff's department parking lot, Quinn sat behind the wheel of her pickup, wondering why in the world she had made the idiotic decision to go there. She should have known what to expect. Of course, Shane would have told the story and shared his concerns. They probably all had a good laugh. Fodder for the gossip mill. She had been so revved up by the coffee and injustice that she hadn't thought it through.

Needing encouragement, she decided to pull up the day's devotional passage and leaned over the center console toward the passenger seat to dig through her bag for her phone. When she finally found it in the bottomless pit of her purse, she straightened back up, her gaze passing across the rearview mirror and the reflection of a man in a ball cap and sunglasses, sitting in the driver's seat of a grey Sonata parked two rows behind her. A chill fluttered down her spine as she froze, taking him in. Even though he wore heavily tinted glasses, there was something in the severity of his posture, his stillness and the pointedness of his stare in her direction that left no doubt in Quinn's mind that he wasn't simply looking at her. He was *watching* her.

As she twisted in her seat to look out the back window for a better view, the driver tore out of the spot, heading for the exit. In seconds he had merged into traffic and sped off down the road.

8

Quinn's very center seemed to vibrate as she pulled out of the sheriff's department parking lot, her heart hammering nervously. It had been months since she felt like someone was watching her like that. Almost exactly six months ago in Tampa. Where everything had fallen apart.

It's nothing, she told herself as she drove to the office, intending to say a quick hello to Terri, drop off the blueberry scone she had picked up for her at The Shed, and grab the gift baskets to deliver to the four rental properties being checked into today. Unfortunately, Terri was extremely chatty, having already heard about the break-in. Quinn's stomach turned at the thought that the gossip mill had already spread the news that far. By dinnertime there wouldn't be a soul left in town who hadn't heard about Quinn Bello hallucinating a dead man on her floor.

Quinn managed to convince Terri that everything was fine, vaguely offering dismissive answers to her not-so-subtle questions about "whether she really thought she saw a body in her house." She also got her to promise that she would *not* contact

47

Quinn's parents about it. She wasn't sure Terri knew that her parents were out of the country on a European river cruise, or how to reach them while they were gone, but she didn't want to risk it. The last thing she needed right now was for her parents to race back to Seaglass Cove, thinking that Quinn couldn't handle things.

When she finally managed to extract herself from Terri's interrogation, she shoved the image of the man watching her to the back of her mind and made the rounds of the rental properties. After ensuring the housekeeping subcontractor was properly cleaning and prepping them, she left a welcome basket on each kitchen counter containing local products—candies, preserves, specialty popcorn and such—along with a handwritten note.

Welcome to Seaglass Cove.
We are so happy you're here!
Enjoy your time in the most peaceful
place on the coast.
Best wishes, Bello Realty

The irony was that, right now, Seaglass Cove felt anything but peaceful to Quinn. After last night, and then today at the sheriff's department, an unease brewed within her. She knew this feeling well. She had shaken hands with it once before. That whisper taunting her. That line of anxiety cast out into the waters of her psyche, just waiting for her to bite and be reeled in—

A blaring horn sounded outside her pickup. Quinn's heart jumped, her eyes going wide as she snapped out of her thoughts, saw a traffic signal rushing toward her and slammed on the brakes, barely avoiding running a red light. Her pulse pounding, she waited for the light to change and her blood pressure to drop, and realized something. What she needed most right then wasn't a cruise in a kayak. It was something else altogether.

~

"I DON'T KNOW what to think, Lena," Quinn said, sitting on a barstool in the kitchen of the Hope Community Center. "This whole thing has really shaken me." After her near accident, Quinn knew what she really needed was to talk things through with someone she trusted. And there was no one she trusted more than Lena Sharp, director of the Center, who also happened to be her friend and accountability partner.

Quinn watched the tall, umber-skinned woman working at one of the stainless steel counters, preparing a large pan of baked chicken for "Open Table" night. Every Saturday night the Center opened its doors to anyone in need of a hot meal: struggling families, the homeless, people out of work, people seeking fellowship—it didn't matter. The Center also tried to identify and meet other needs, including offering a weekly substance abuse recovery group led by Lena, open to anyone who could use the support. Anyone like Quinn.

One of the first things Quinn's parents did when she landed back in Seaglass Cove five months ago was to connect her with the Hope Recovery Group. Because the Center was a ministry operated by their church—it was located on the lot next door—her parents often volunteered at the Center and were familiar with its programs. Quinn resisted at first but now couldn't be more grateful that they insisted she try it.

In addition to attending the group, Quinn also volunteered at the Center as her parents had done. On Mondays she helped assemble dozens of boxes containing a month's worth of groceries for those in need. On Saturdays she often helped out with the Open Table cooking and serving. Occasionally she even taught classes as part of the Women's Job Training

Program on Thursday nights. Her service at the Center was incredibly humbling and such a privilege, and one of her favorite things about living in Seaglass Cove again. The true friend she had found in Lena was an added blessing.

Lena was one of those striking beauties, someone who could have easily graced the cover of Vogue, if given the chance. She was lanky, with cheekbones like the edge of a cliff and dark-brown eyes offset by ridiculously long lashes. In her early twenties, life had not been kind to Lena, leaving her a widow with two young children. After a series of further hardships, she eventually found herself homeless and an alcoholic. A concerned friend connected her with the Hope Community Center where she found both hope and recovery. Now, five years later, Lena was running the Center and using the broken-ness she had been healed of to bring healing and comfort to others. Lena was the only person in Seaglass Cove who truly understood the depths of the pit Quinn had been in, the cost of climbing out, and the struggle to build something again.

"You had a break-in," Lena said, as she jiggled small jars of spices over the chicken, seasoning it with salt, pepper, thyme and rosemary. "Of course you're rattled. That's understandable."

Quinn hadn't told Lena about the dead body, only that someone broke into the house. Even as much as she trusted Lena, after Shane's reaction and the reaction of the deputies at the station, she couldn't help wondering whether Lena would believe her, or doubt like Shane, thinking that she simply misinterpreted the situation. Or worse, think that Quinn was seeing things that weren't there. Like before.

She would tell Lena all of it eventually, but not right now. "That guy in the parking lot...and the sensation that he was watching me. It was so strong. It felt like Tampa, Lena. That same certainty."

Lena stopped covering the pan with foil and looked up, her

eyes narrowed thoughtfully. "Is there any reason other than the break-in that could explain why you might be feeling like this?"

"No," Quinn answered emphatically, her heart shrinking. She knew what Lena meant. She was asking if she had slipped. Taken something. Started drinking again. Even though she knew it was Lena's job as her accountability partner to ask, it was still a kick to the gut. Lena nodded and resumed sealing the foil around the pan. She seemed to take Quinn at her word, which at least softened the blow a little bit.

"What did the police say?" Lena asked as she carried the finished pan to the commercial-sized refrigerator, trailing the aroma of rosemary and thyme as she passed Quinn.

"Are you sure I can't help you?" Quinn asked, sliding off the stool. "Can I start something...the green beans, maybe?"

"Uh-uh," Lena declined, as she walked back to the counter, grabbed another pan of chicken, and pointed a commanding finger at Quinn. "You sit. Talk. I've got this."

Twinges of guilt pinched Quinn as she sat idle, watching Lena work. It felt wrong not pitching in. "Shane said they would look into it, but his guess is that it was a burglary gone wrong. But the problem with that theory is that nothing was missing."

"Maybe they heard you coming and left before they could do any damage."

"Maybe." Quinn said, biting her lip. She still didn't buy it.

Lena braced her slender hands on the counter, her eyes full of compassion. "I think that after what you experienced last night, it's understandable you would be hyper-aware today. I think seeing this man watching you in the parking lot brought back feelings tied to one of the worst days of your life. Like muscle memory, only in this case emotional memory."

Quinn's churning nerves settled a little. Lena had a point.

"I mean, you didn't go after him, chase him down, yell at him or anything, did you?" Lena asked.

A sad pang struck Quinn as the memory of doing exactly that to the man in her parking garage in Tampa flashed in her mind. "No."

"And you didn't see anyone else watching or following you, right? I mean, it's not a pattern. You're not seeing people spying around every corner."

That's true, I'm not. "No."

Lena inclined her head toward Quinn. "So there you go. You're not overreacting. You're not escalating like before."

Another worker entered the kitchen through a swinging door, heading for the refrigerator. Lena stopped speaking, waiting until after he got what he needed and left before continuing. "Have you called Dr. Bristol?"

Quinn shook her head. "I wanted to talk to you first." In truth, she didn't want to call her psychiatrist at all. Not if she could help it. It would feel too much like heading back down a road she never wanted to travel again.

"What about your mom and dad? What do they say?"

"I, um, haven't told them," Quinn answered hesitantly.

Lena's head pivoted toward Quinn, her face wrinkled in consternation. "Why in the world not? You know they'd want to know."

"Because if they know, they'll start to worry and they'll come right back here. I'm finally getting on my feet. I don't want them concerned or second-guessing their decision to leave."

Or second-guessing me. She didn't like to think about whether her parents would believe her or side with Shane. It would hurt so much if they doubted her.

"Well, look," Lena said. "I think you just got spooked. Get some rest tonight and I really think you'll feel better in the morning." She jerked her head at the sack beside Quinn marked with The Little Red Shed's logo. "What'cha got there?"

"Oh! I brought something for you," Quinn said, lifting the bag. "Well, full disclosure, it was for Terri, but I was so flustered when I left the office I forgot to give it to her. You like blueberry scones, right?"

A wide grin broke out on Lena's face. "Who doesn't?" she asked, and after putting the last pan of chicken in the fridge, snatched the bag from Quinn. She dug out the scone, popped a chunk in her mouth, and leaned against the counter next to Quinn's stool. "My hips don't much care for them, but the rest of me has a different opinion."

Quinn laughed.

"So you saw Ian Wolfe again today," Lena asked, a knowing glint in her eye.

"What do you mean, 'again'?" Quinn replied, crossing her arms.

"I mean the last time you were here you mentioned you'd been by there for lunch. The time before that it was breakfast."

"So? I like the food." A faint heat began creeping across Quinn's collarbone.

"I think the food's not the only thing you like."

Quinn playfully snatched the remainder of the scone from Lena's hand. "I think you need to mind your own business."

"What would be the fun in that?" Lena asked, raising her eyebrows and holding her hand out expectantly until Quinn dropped the scone back in it.

"I'm not interested in Ian Wolfe," Quinn protested, shaking her head. "I'm just getting my life back on track."

"Mm-hmm."

"I don't need the complications."

"Mm-hmm."

"And I tend to be trouble. He doesn't need that. No one does."

Lena eyed Quinn intensely. "Don't you go limiting yourself like that."

"Well, it's true," Quinn asserted.

"What's true about your past doesn't have to be the truth of your future."

Quinn shrugged. "It doesn't matter anyway. He's interested in someone. Or at least I think he is."

"You sound pretty observant about his situation for someone who isn't interested," Lena said, her words thick with irony.

Quinn stared Lena down. "Aren't you too busy to be sticking your nose into my love life—or lack of one?"

Lena glanced at her arm, pretending to check a watch that didn't exist, then looked up defiantly. "Nope."

9

Quinn's visit with Lena definitely made her feel better. But by the time she left the Center, after ultimately pitching in to help with the green beans and rolls, and then serving, it was six thirty. There wasn't enough time before sunset to go kayaking, and anyway, she was pretty drained. Even though she was dying to get out on the water, rest was probably a better prescription than paddling at the moment.

But however much she wanted to head straight home and curl up with a good book, she still hadn't been to the grocery store. Which meant her fridge was empty. The thought of strolling grocery aisles only magnified her exhaustion, so when she saw The Shed coming up on the right as she drove home, she made a quick turn into the lot. On Saturdays it was open till nine, the only day it offered dinner. She could grab some takeout and have a nice, quiet meal on her back porch.

And stopping here has nothing to do with Ian Wolfe, Lena. I'm just hungry.

The place was packed. Saturday nights were the busiest evenings for The Shed, when lots of groups held their events—

painting, crafting, whatever—or just gathered to hang out and listen to the live music. Tonight a three-piece jazz band was playing a Sinatra standard, the double bassist plucking away, sending out a deep, mellow sound that wrapped itself around Quinn as she stepped inside.

She glanced over at the counter and saw that one of Ian's employees was working the register. Mild disappointment stung her, and she tried not to imagine the smug expression Lena would be wearing if she knew. She stepped back from the counter, craning her neck to scan the area in front of the stage. *Maybe he's just in another part of the—*

"Looking for someone?"

The voice was rich and warm, came from the reading area behind her, and she knew before she looked that it was him. She hoped her face wasn't as flushed as it felt. And if it was, that he wouldn't notice.

She turned, an amused smile slipping onto his face as he cocked his head.

So much for him not noticing.

"Hey, stranger," he said.

"Hey," she answered. He had changed from that morning and now wore dark jeans and a grey button-down. The wet, white cloth he twisted in his hands suggested she had interrupted him while wiping down tables.

"So you're back? Twice in one day," he noted.

Lena's teasing about Ian came back to her. "Guess I'm becoming a nuisance," she said, and immediately regretted that she sounded a little defensive. Lena had really gotten into her head.

"No, it's a good thing," he spouted quickly, apparently picking up on the edge in her voice. "I'm glad. I mean, what would we do without repeat customers?"

"True," she said, and favored him with a smile, hoping to

brush away any awkwardness. "Anyway, I'm just grabbing something to take home."

"Ahh. Still no groceries, huh?"

She chuckled, remembering that she shared that tidbit with him a couple of weeks ago. "Nope. The chore keeps getting pushed further down the to-do list."

"Well, as much as I like having you in here all the time, we can't risk you starving to death at home. Maybe we could—"

"Quinn?"

This time the voice came from the entryway, and Quinn turned to see Shane Cody walking toward her. "I saw your truck in the lot. The office said you came in today."

"Yeah," she answered, as Ian discreetly stepped a few yards away and started wiping down a table.

"I thought the least I could do was stop in and update you." Shane ran a hand over his head and shifted his feet. He looked uncomfortable. "They said you didn't have anything to report. That nothing was missing."

"No. Nothing."

"Well, that's good." His tone didn't sound like he thought it was good, though.

"Is it? Because it makes it feel less like a robbery and more like an invasion. And it doesn't explain the body on my floor."

Maybe it was all in her head, but it seemed like a vacuum suddenly sucked the sound out of the immediate area. Though she didn't turn to check, Quinn got the distinct impression that Ian had stopped working.

"There wasn't a dead body," Shane stated firmly, his face clouding. "We searched the whole area, Quinn. We didn't find anything. And there were no reports this morning about anyone seeing anything strange in the vicinity last night."

Quinn sighed. "I don't want to do this again. I know what I saw."

Shane put his hands on his hips. "You're really not gonna let this go? Quinn, if you saw somebody on your floor—"

"If?" She could hear the jump in her pitch that matched the jump in her body tension, her neck and chest now noticeably tight.

"That's not what I meant. I just meant that I still think whoever you saw was either playing like he was knocked out, or actually had been knocked out by an accomplice, then regained consciousness and left while you were gone. You're making this into something more sinister than it is."

"As in, I'm seeing things?" Her skin prickled, the hairs rising on her arms.

Shane sighed. "Noooo," he said, drawing the 'no' out, aggravating Quinn even more. "Not seeing things. Just misconstruing them."

Quinn swallowed hard, straining to keep her tone even despite the ire mounting within. "So what now?"

"We've increased patrols in the area for the next few nights, just in case."

"And that's it?" she asked, her words sharp.

"There's nothing else to do."

Anger flashed through her like wildfire, and Quinn bit her lip to keep from saying something she would regret.

"Just use your alarm, all right?" he asked.

She nodded, willing him to go. She had never wanted to see the back of anyone more in her entire life.

QUINN CONTINUED STARING at the door after it closed behind Shane, the cowbell suspended above it cheerfully clanking as he exited.

"Um, did I hear you say 'body'?"

Quinn turned back to Ian who was still standing near the

table he had been cleaning, the cloth now balled up in his hands.

"Uh, yeah." Her stomach curdled. She hated that he knew this now.

"You didn't say anything about a body this morning."

Quinn tried to wipe her face of emotion, feigning apathy. "Didn't want to get into it." *Don't want to get into it now, either.*

"Why does it sound like he doesn't believe you?"

Quinn huffed. "Because he doesn't." She hesitated, then wagged her head back and forth. "Well, not completely."

"Why in the world wouldn't he believe you?" Ian asked, his brow scrunched up.

Quinn glanced around the reading area. Only one other person occupied it, and she was curled up in a cushy chair on the opposite side at least fifteen feet away, with her nose in a thick book. The band was loud. Everybody else was either near the stage or working in other spaces. She was going to chance it.

"Because by the time the sheriff's department got to the house, the body had disappeared," she explained, keeping her voice low.

Ian's head jutted forward as he splayed his hands and let loose an incredulous laugh. "So? What difference does that make?"

Quinn's heart melted at his indignation over the notion that Shane hadn't believed her, even though the facts—no body and no corroborating evidence it ever existed—all supported Shane. She knew that if Ian knew her history—specifically the experiences that birthed Shane's enduring skepticism—he might rethink his reaction. But she didn't care. It was just wonderful, for once, to have someone believe her without a second thought. She offered him a grin, her gaze locked into his deep, dark eyes.

"What is it?" he asked, the corner of his mouth turning up,

apparently thrown by her somewhat disproportionate reaction to his display of annoyance. When she didn't answer, he pressed her. "Quinn, why wouldn't he believe you?"

I suppose there's no way around it now, she thought and exhaled slowly, her breath hissing from her lungs as her eyebrows rose.

"How much time have you got?"

10

They sat at the table Ian had been cleaning, a narrow two-seater pressed against the window, empty but for the salt and pepper shakers. Quinn ran a hand along the buttery-smooth sanded top made of reclaimed wood, stalling. Ian leaned on it, his arms crossed in front of him, sending the scent of sandalwood floating in her direction. Finally, she looked up at him and started in.

"I was only twelve at the time," Quinn said, dropping her hands into her lap. "We'd lived here my whole life. There were four of us who ran around together. Me, Jess, Gina and Annie. For the most part, we stayed out of trouble. But Jess had a mischievous side and liked to push it. So when I started going through a bit of a rebellious phase, she was more than happy to indulge me."

Ian's right eyebrow arched. "What kind of rebellious phase? How bad could it have been? I'll bet you were just adorably precocious."

"I wish that's all it was. I'd always been the good one. Good grades. Good behavior. Good girl in church every Sunday. My dad was a deacon. But then I started getting teased about it in school. And I was a little awkward, this pale kid with wild red hair, six inches taller than most of the boys. Being good was the one thing I could change, so I started acting out."

"Acting out how?"

Quinn's gaze left Ian's face and she looked off toward the stage, allowing the memories to surface from their shadows. "At first I just started taking things from stores. A pack of gum here, a candy bar there, lip gloss, whatever. I lied about how I got it whenever Mom would stumble across something. Then one day I got caught and they had to come down to the drugstore to get me. It was horrible."

"I'll bet."

"This is a small town now, but it was even smaller back then. It didn't take long for word to get out."

His face wrinkled in sympathy. "That must've been awful."

A wry smile creased Quinn's lips. "Actually, I loved it because the kids at school thought it was awesome. My stock in the seventh grade skyrocketed."

"Which only made you want to do it more."

She nodded, her eyes squeezed shut in contrition. "I actually felt pretty guilty about hurting my parents, but I didn't want to lose my notoriety. I was on the verge of being one of the 'popular' kids. So, on the rare occasions when I wasn't already grounded, I'd find ways to make trouble—egging houses, mixing up people's mail, cheating on tests so I didn't have to work so hard. I would lie until I got caught, then beg forgiveness."

"Let me see if I have this straight," Ian said, an unmistakeable note of cynicism in his voice. "You're telling me that this cop doesn't believe you because you had a difficult streak when you were twelve?"

Quinn sighed and rubbed a hand over her mouth. She wasn't going to be able to avoid this part, as much as she might want to. She leaned on her forearms, mirroring Ian. "One night, the four of us had a sleepover at Gina's house. Or at least we were supposed to. We were watching this movie about some high school kids who followed through on a dare to get attention. I got the bright idea that we should do something like it and proposed we make a Ten Tree Island run."

"As in the island the lighthouse sits on, right out there?" Ian asked, slinging a finger in the general direction of the coast.

Quinn nodded, feeling a familiar queasiness at the mention of the tiny island. It was small, but its memory packed a punch. One hundred yards at its widest point, it had only enough room for about ten long-leaf pines—hence its name—and the lighthouse built in 1891, which was no longer operational. It was positioned a mile off the coast of Seaglass Cove, separating the waters of the St. John Sound from the Gulf of Mexico.

Quinn breathed in through her nose, ignoring the threatening churn of her stomach and kept going. "There was this stupid ongoing challenge for teens to kayak over there in the dark, snap a photo next to the lighthouse and get back without being busted by the coastal patrol."

"Sounds like a typical, idiotic high school stunt."

"Yeah. Well, it was pretty dangerous. All kinds of boats cut through the sound even in the middle of the night. But while the boats have lights—"

"Kayaks don't," he finished for her.

"Exactly. The four of us didn't have a way to get our kayaks to the shore, but Gina lived near the water so we could walk. There was a cove with this old rowboat that had been there forever. I don't even know who it belonged to, but I suggested we row it to the island using our kayak paddles and then we'd have an awesome story with the photos to prove it."

"So what happened?"

"We decided to go around midnight. But the closer it got, the more scared I was. I got cold feet. I said we should forget it and Jess started teasing me, calling me a baby. I left with my stuff and rode my bike home. I surprised my parents by showing up around ten. They fussed at me for riding so late by myself, but I told them I'd had a fight with the other girls and just wanted to be home. I went straight to bed. About two and half hours later they woke me up, telling me that my friends had disappeared from Gina's place and that all the parents were scared to death."

"Did you tell them what you knew?"

Quinn rubbed the back of her neck, the bony finger of shame poking her insides. "No. I didn't want to be a snitch. I may not have gone through with the dare, but I wasn't going to get my friends in trouble. I would have never lived that down. I was twelve and stupid and couldn't imagine something actually going wrong. Tons of kids had been pulling the run off for years without a hitch."

"That's hard to believe," Ian said as the band reached a crescendo, their slow jazz number swelling throughout the space.

"Well, at least we hadn't *heard* about anyone getting hurt."

"So what happened?"

"I lied and told my parents I had no idea where the girls were. Then around two in the morning we got the call. They'd been in a boating accident with a commercial fisherman. He collided with them. Didn't even see their boat before he hit it. The thing split into pieces and capsized."

Ian sucked in a soft gasp. "Oh, Quinn."

"Yeah. They were all wearing life jackets, thank goodness, and Gina and Jess weren't hurt, just waterlogged. But Annie got the worst of it. His boat hit theirs on her side. She ended up with a spinal injury. She recovered eventually, but it took five years of therapy to get her walking again."

"Oh, wow. Quinn, that's terrible."

"Yeah. And it was my fault."

He pushed up slightly on his forearms, leaning back a bit. "How do you figure that?"

"At the time my parents woke me, the girls would have just made it to the water, or at least just pushed in. If I had told the truth right away, they could have gotten to them in time. But because I lied, they were able to get halfway out into the sound, which is where they lost their paddles when a wave hit, and ended up stranded out there, just floating."

"You were twelve. And you tried to change their minds."

"Well, it was my idea and my lie that kept them out there. That's how their parents saw it, anyway. And the town. I was an outcast for a long time. Eventually people calmed down but I'd been labeled. I was untrustworthy. A liar."

"Quinn, I'm so sorry."

She drew her lips into a taut line and bobbed her head once before quickly continuing, not wanting to linger in his pity. "After that, I straightened up. Tried to shake the label, but it never felt like I did, partly because I believed I deserved it."

"What about Annie? Did she hold it against you?"

Quinn pursed her lips. "Oddly enough, she was one of the few people who forgave me. Insisted it *wasn't* my fault. She was solid, Annie. Deep faith for a twelve-year-old."

"And that story is the reason why Deputy Cody won't believe you? Because you had a lying problem when you were twelve?"

Quinn dipped her head before looking back up at him from beneath her eyelashes. "Well, the thing is, Annie's last name is Cody too. She's his cousin."

"Oh," Ian said, understanding in his tone.

"Yeah. He wasn't quite as forgiving as Annie, nor was the rest of her family. They eventually moved away. I haven't seen her since. Couldn't even bring myself to ask him about her the other night. I can't stand the way he used to look at me when her name would come up. I didn't want to see that again. I don't want to see myself through his eyes. I already feel like enough of a failure."

Ian watched her for a moment, then sniffed. "Gimme a minute," he said, sliding out of his chair and heading into the kitchen.

Quinn watched him go, then let her eyes drift across the room. White string lights, suspended in a zig-zag pattern above the stage and wound around several potted trees, created a cozy atmosphere that complemented the jazz vibe. Laughter and a low buzz of voices mixed with the music made the place seem cheerful. Happy. People were having a good time. It was no wonder they came here. In just a few months, Ian had managed to turn The Shed into "the place" to be. It wasn't surprising. He was warm and inviting and easy to talk to. People seemed naturally drawn to him, so of course they would naturally be drawn to his place.

It also didn't surprise her that he excused himself after she told him about the accident. Whenever she found herself in the position of having to recount it, she always sensed that people looked at her differently once they heard the story. She wasn't sure if it was just in her head or not, but it felt true enough.

She always worried that, like Shane did, other people would hold her past against her. That it would shape their perception of her—be a lens they would look through in judging her and that it would ultimately diminish her value in their eyes. That it would, on some level, define for them who she was at her core. Once a liar, always a liar.

Is that what Ian's thinking now?

And if not, would he be, once he heard the rest of her story?

11

The sound of a plate clanking down in front of Quinn jerked her out of her reverie. She looked away from a couple dancing to "Fly Me to the Moon," to see a plate of chicken salad, a croissant, greens with poppyseed dressing and pasta salad.

Ian set a glass of water beside the plate and slid into his seat again, clutching a wide-brimmed mug of tea. Notes of bergamot from what she suspected was Earl Grey wafted across the table.

"What's this?" she asked, pointing to the plate.

He looked at her like she was asking him why he was breathing. "You came in here for dinner. I figured you were getting hungry. Can't have you confessing your life's sins on an empty stomach, can we?"

She snorted softly. "Guess not." She took a bite and like everything he served, it was delicious and unique. "What is that in the chicken salad—cayenne pepper?"

"Gives it that little kick."

She nodded and took a sip of water. There was definitely a kick.

"So here's the thing," he said, gripping his mug with lean fingers that had a rugged quality to them. "I still don't get it. I understand Cody's got an issue with you, but it's been...what... fifteen years?"

She smiled faintly. It was always nice when people underestimated your age. "Eighteen."

"Okay, eighteen. How could he possibly hold that against you in this situation, and this long after? If you say you saw a body, why wouldn't he take you seriously?"

She stabbed a pasta bowtie and lifted the fork to her mouth, the olive oil, vinegar, and cilantro tangy on her tongue. She swallowed. "Because there's more you don't know," she said, hearing the trepidation in her voice.

As soon as she said it, suspicion flared within her. Why didn't he know the rest of it? He had been in Seaglass Cove long enough for the town's legendary gossip mill to reach him. In fact, why didn't he know everything already?

"Hold on," she said, setting her fork down, now wondering if he was taking her for a ride—persuading her to tell him things he already knew. "Have you really never heard the boat story, or anything else...questionable...about me before now?"

He finished the sip he was taking from his mug and set it on the table with a thunk. "Nope."

"Because I find it hard to believe that the town's chatter hasn't reached The Shed. You've been here, what, six months?"

"I've got a strict no-gossip policy."

"Seriously?"

"Seriously." He eyed her appraisingly, as if deciding whether or not to tell her something. "If you really want to know, there have been a couple of people who saw you in here and, after you left, they tried to bring you up. They started in on an old story or began hinting at the reasons why you came back, but I shut them down."

Quinn tried to imagine how a person telling a story like that would react if Ian had actually stopped them in their tracks. It would have been pretty amusing. "A strict no-gossip policy, huh?" she asked, feeling the corner of her mouth pull up.

The granite expression on his face said he was dead serious. "If I'm not part of the problem or part of the solution, I figure I don't need to know it."

"That's pretty noble of you."

"I don't know about noble, but I do know it's hard enough to get through life without people pointing out your mistakes to everyone else."

"You're not wrong about that." She folded her hands in her lap and scooted to the edge of her seat. "The thing with Annie devastated me. Changed me. It made me want to be better. To do better. I promised myself I would spend my life doing good for people, not hurting them. I decided I wanted to stand up for people who had been hurt, help them get justice. I went to law school, then to work for a plaintiffs' firm in Tampa, representing people who were disadvantaged or damaged somehow."

"Sounds like you were working hard to make amends."

"I was, but it was stressful. Sometimes there were millions of dollars at stake. We represented the injured, widows, widowers, orphans, people victimized by fraud—the list was varied and endless. While it felt really good to help people, the eighty-hour workweeks started to take their toll. And if I'm honest, at some point the success and money eclipsed the desire to make a difference. I was aiming to make partner too, so I just kept piling it on. I started having anxiety attacks, small at first, then full blown panic episodes. And," she paused, for some reason feeling awkward about mentioning this part, "I was engaged. Simon was a resident at a hospital in Tampa. But my job and his job and my growing anxiety started eating away at our relationship. He didn't like that the hours I was working conflicted with his or the way it was consuming me—and as a resident he had his own stuff going on. We almost never saw each other."

"Eventually I started self-medicating to take the edge off. A drink here and there...but it didn't help. I started having crying fits. It became hard to get out of bed. I began missing deadlines, I was late all the time and I was lying to everyone in the office, trying to hide my condition. Finally Simon pushed me to see a psychiatrist, and talking about it did help. She prescribed alprazolam and that helped too. For a little while. But then my workload got even heavier and Simon and I were fighting and it wasn't enough. I went back to the doctor and she prescribed something else and that seemed to make a real difference, until it didn't. There were days when it got so hard to push through. I felt like I couldn't breathe. So occasionally I drank on top of the medication, hoping to even myself out."

"I know that didn't work."

"No. But by that time, the panic was getting so bad I wasn't thinking straight. Finally I started taking the alprazolam on top of the other med, hoping that would do it. I was in this spiral of lying and self-medicating and working myself to the bone and everything was falling apart. And then I started to suspect someone was watching me."

"What, like, stalking you?"

Quinn nodded. "Exactly like stalking me. I would get this feeling—walking to my car or into my condo—that somebody was following me. I'd see shadows move but no one was there. I'd go to my office late at night and feel a presence. I'd go in and out of rooms searching for someone, because I just knew they were there."

"But you never found anyone," Ian said.

She wagged her head. "No. The panic kept growing and I never slept. My heart raced constantly and I was having palpitations—PVCs, you know, where your heart skips? It happens if I get too worked up. Simon was threatening to end the engagement. It finally all came to a head one day when I was in a courtroom waiting for a hearing to start. I thought someone had been stalking me in the parking garage, and I'd seen a man by the elevators who I thought was watching me. Then in the courtroom I heard someone call my name and there was the same man, coming at me, reaching into his pocket, pulling out a gun. There was a deputy near me and I took *his* gun and fired on the man before he could shoot me or anyone else."

Ian's eyebrows were arched toward the ceiling, astonishment splashed across his face. "That's...unbelievable. It sounds like you saved a lot of people."

Quinn frowned. "No. Turned out, there was no gun. It was just a guy with a cell phone. And he wasn't even there for me— he was the plaintiff in another case."

Ian's mouth dropped open. "What happened?"

"Nobody got hurt. Fortunately, in my state I was a terrible shot. Put two holes in the wall before the deputy took me down."

"What about you hearing your name called? What was that?"

"Didn't happen. I hallucinated it. Along with the shadows moving and constantly sensing someone following me. The doctor's final diagnosis was that the combination of anxiety, stress, no sleep, alcohol, and doubling up on the medications put me in a state of paranoia which led to the hallucinations."

"Wow."

Quinn expelled a small, sad huff. "Yeah. The fallout dragged on for a few months, but long-story-short, I was disbarred." She made air quotes as she said, "For engaging in an intentional abuse of prescribed medications and alcoholic substances leading to actions which constituted an assault on multiple persons, recklessly endangering lives and resulting in a conviction of one count of simple assault." Quinn recited the precise wording of her disbarment notice with robotic efficiency, having read the language enough times to commit it to memory. But the repetition had done nothing to diminish its sting.

"They convicted you of a crime? With you in that state of mind?"

Quinn's gaze shifted as she rubbed her thumb up and down her glass. "I was abusing substances. I wasn't in my right mind by the end, but I made the decision to take what I took. My attorney was able to get the charges knocked down to simple assault because of the mental capacity question, so I avoided jail time. But the state bar wasn't so forgiving."

"And so you came home?"

"The courtroom thing happened in November. By the end of December I had pled guilty to simple assault and was put on probation with the condition of completing rehab. I came here for Christmas, then went into rehab for thirty days. The bar's decision came down right after I completed my program, so in early February I packed up, left Tampa and came here to live with my parents. They had been wanting to retire and I needed a job so I took over the realty business. By March they felt like I could handle it, and moved to Delray Beach. And that is the story of me."

She leaned back from the table, drained after spilling the whole sordid tale. Aside from Lena, Ian was the first person Quinn had shared the whole ugly truth with. Her nerves hummed as she waited to see how he would take it.

He reached out, putting a hand on her forearm, his skin warm with the mug's heat. "No. That's not the story of you, Quinn. It's just one of your stories."

"What's the difference?"

"It's the difference between something being your definition and something being one of your defining moments."

She wasn't sure she bought into that, but she appreciated what he was trying to do. "Well, whatever it is, combined with what happened when I was twelve, it's the reason that Shane Cody won't give me the benefit of the doubt. I'm not sure if he thinks I'm confused, or self-medicating again and hallucinating or just flat-out lying. But he doesn't believe me and neither do the people he works with, based on the reception I got there today. On top of that, this morning when I got to work, my office manager had already heard about the entire episode."

"How did it get to her that fast?"

Quinn almost laughed at the sincere surprise on his face. He may have lived in Seaglass Cove for months, but he still didn't appreciate its capacity for rumor mongering. "Tiny town. Word travels fast. Her best friend is a woman whose husband is in the sheriff's department, and right now I'm juicy gossip. Anyway, she was hinting around, asking if I was feeling overwhelmed, had I maybe done anything to take the edge off? And she won't be the only one asking those questions. By tonight most of the town will know and think I'm off the wagon again."

"Quinn, based on what you've told me, it sounds like you're in recovery and doing all right with that. Are you?"

His forthrightness surprised her, but she didn't find it annoying. At least he wasn't tiptoeing around her, making vague insinuations. "I am."

"You're not relapsing? Not drinking, not abusing medication?"

"No. I'm not even on the meds anymore. They work some people, but didn't for me."

"Okay. Then you know the truth and you have to cling to that. And as for Cody, unless he's got evidence that you made the body up, he's got an obligation to pursue it whether you're relapsing or not. If you ask me, he's letting a personal bias get in the way."

"I can't really blame him, given our history."

"Well, that aside, let me ask you something. Those hallucinations you were having before—did you actually see something that wasn't there?"

Quinn searched her memory. "It was more like I misinterpreted things. Thought shadows were more than they were. Stuff like that. I did hear things that didn't happen—"

"But you didn't see things that weren't there?"

"No. The man in the courtroom didn't have a gun, but he *was* pulling out a black cell phone."

"Okay, so, if you didn't see things that weren't there back in Tampa, why should Cody think you hallucinated a dead guy on your floor?"

"Well, I'm not sure he thinks that, exactly. I think he believes I mistook an unconscious man on my floor as a dead one."

Ian tapped the fingers of one hand on the table. "Something doesn't add up here. Walk me through what happened last night step-by-step and don't leave out a thing."

12

"And that's all of it," Quinn said, as she finished recounting the break-in for Ian. "You heard Shane —with nothing taken and no leads there's basically nothing to do."

Ian hunched over the table, his hands folded in front of him, fingers interlaced. He had pushed his mug aside and for several minutes now had been rolling his thumbs over each other as he listened to her talk. He said nothing the whole time, alternating his intense stare between her and his own hands. His gaze was so pointed that a few times when he locked eyes with her, Quinn's stomach did a little flip.

"Before last night, had you ever felt you were being watched since coming back to Seaglass Cove?"

"No. Never."

"Well, I think he's got this all wrong."

A wave of heady disbelief rolled over her. "You believe me?"

"Absolutely."

"Why? You don't even know me."

Ian straightened in his seat, dropping his broad shoulders. "Because I think people deserve a second chance. There's no reason to believe that anything you've said isn't true, other than evaluating it based on your past, and I just don't think that's right. People make mistakes. But that doesn't mean we should automatically judge everything they do by those mistakes. Mistakes are something we do. They aren't who we are."

He was talking to her, but there was a fervor in his tone that suggested his comments weren't just about her. *What's your story, Ian Wolfe?* she thought.

Before she had time to ponder the question further, he plunged ahead with one of his own. "Was there anything strange, anything that seemed off to you when you first walked back in your place and found the guy on the floor?"

"You mean, other than the guy on the floor?" she asked, feeling the corners of her mouth draw up.

He laughed. "Yeah, other than that."

Quinn let her gaze wander off into the growing number of people milling about the dance floor as she scrolled through the mental images of what she had seen that night. After a few moments, she looked back at him.

"You know, there was. He was dressed in khakis and a button-down shirt. He looked more like a copy store clerk than a burglar. It didn't make sense to me. I even told Shane, but he didn't think much of it."

"That is pretty odd. What about his shoes?"

"His shoes?"

Ian nodded, his eyebrows rising expectantly.

Quinn's brow furrowed as she tried to remember. "I'm not sure. Dockers, I think? Or something similar."

Ian bit his lower lip. "I agree with you. That just doesn't sound like a burglar to me. What about aside from that night? Is there anything strange going on in your world? Weird things you've noticed? If this guy wasn't a run-of-the-mill burglar, then he was there for some other reason."

"Well," she started hesitantly, "okay, there is something. But you might think I'm just being paranoid."

"Try me," he said.

Quinn inhaled a deep breath, her posture sinking as she let it out. "Today when I was leaving the sheriff's department parking lot—after I went in to try to see Shane—I noticed this car parked behind me. And I thought...I thought the driver was watching me."

"What made you think that?" Ian didn't sound skeptical. He sounded curious.

"Just the *way* he was staring in my direction. He did have sunglasses on, but you know how you can tell when someone's looking at you? Plus, the minute he caught me eyeing him, he drove off."

"Sounds like you could be right."

No protest? No, 'you're just imagining things'? She wasn't used to being afforded this kind of credibility. "Wait, you really think he was watching me?"

"I don't know. But I wouldn't rule it out. Anything else happen lately?"

She thought about it. "I had some hang-up calls a few weeks ago."

He leaned forward again, cocking his head. "What kind of calls?"

"Just numbers I didn't recognize and no one answering on the other end. I assumed they were telemarketing calls, you know, the kind where it takes a little while for the call to connect? So I just stopped answering numbers I didn't know. Some hung up, others went to voicemail but they never left a message. I thought my number had ended up on a list somewhere."

"Did you ever get calls from the same number?"

"Initially. Until I started blocking them," she replied.

"Huh. Did you ever try calling them back?" he asked.

"No, why would I?"

The stage area was really hopping now and most of the other spaces were filling up too. Another couple of readers had wandered into the sitting area, and one man was pecking away on his laptop at a nearby table.

"Should you get back to it?" Quinn asked, waving a hand at the room. "You've been hanging out with me for a while."

"Nah. I've got extra help on Saturday nights," he said, and swiveled to look back at the counter, where a teenager was taking orders while another employee carried a food-laden tray into the pottery area. He turned back to Quinn, a sparkle in his eye as he dramatically lowered his voice. "I'm all yours."

Although she could tell he was teasing her, his husky tone still had a discombobulating effect. "Uh... okay," she answered, hoping she didn't sound like the freshman who just got winked at by the senior quarterback.

If she did, Ian ignored it, instead launching into more questions. "What if the calls weren't telemarketers? What if someone was trying to reach you?"

"Then why wouldn't they say anything when I picked up? Or leave a message?"

"Nerves maybe? Second-guessing themselves? Maybe they eventually got over it, but by then you had decided not to answer. It might explain why a stranger showed up at your house unannounced."

"But not why he was dead on my floor."

"No. Can you think of anyone who would need to reach you, but keep it quiet? Or anyone with a grudge against you? What about old clients—or unhappy opponents on the other side?"

"I don't think any of my clients would do that," she said. "And if someone on the opposition wanted to threaten me, I doubt they'd just call and hang up."

"Probably not." Ian wrapped his hands around his mug

again, even though it was empty now, tapping the side with one finger. "I don't like it. If you say this guy was dead—"

"He was. I know dead. This guy was gone."

"Then keep at it. He was in your house for a reason. I'm not saying you should be scared, but I'm saying you need to follow this up and figure it out if you can."

"I'm not sure if that makes me feel better or worse."

"Check in with your old firm, see if anyone's been asking about you. And maybe at your place in Tampa? And what about your fiancé?"

"Ex-fiancé," she answered, feeling the familiar tightening around her heart. It wasn't sadness exactly. More like disappointment.

"Oh. I'm sorry," he apologized, his expression troubled.

"It's okay. It was just one of those things. He couldn't handle the substance abuse issue, him being a resident on the rise and all. Didn't want it to mar his reputation."

Sour distaste crinkled Ian's deep-set, slate-grey eyes. "He just abandoned you?"

"Oh," she said, sighing resignedly, "I think we abandoned each other long before what happened in that courtroom. I was lying about how I was managing my anxiety and taking pills and the rest. And he was too busy to get to the bottom of why, or invest in helping me overcome it. It wasn't meant to be."

"Sounds like a lucky escape if you ask me."

She chuckled softly. "That's what my dad said," she replied, then yawned, quickly throwing a hand up to cover it.

"You're exhausted," Ian said, then checked his watch, an old classic, not a smartwatch, with a simple black leather strap. "It's only seven forty-five, though."

She wrinkled her nose. "No sleep last night. Burglar, remember? Dead body?"

He clicked his tongue. "Right," he said, then nodded at the

half-full plate in front of her. "I can wrap that up for you. You should head home, try to get some rest."

"That's probably a good idea." The thought of crawling into bed sounded like heaven.

"And, Quinn, use your alarm, okay? Cody was right about that." There was an urgency in his tone that made it clear this was more than a suggestion.

"I will."

"But forget what he said about there being nothing more you can do. You should keep looking," he encouraged her. "See if you can find anything that might make him take you more seriously."

"I will. Thanks for listening. And for believing me."

"Thanks for trusting me with your story."

A sudden bit of daring seized her. "You know, something tells me that I'm not the only one with a story."

He had risen from his chair and reached for her plate, but at her words he paused, leaving him positioned much closer to Quinn than before. A charge surged in the space between them as he seemed to consider her comment, but his face remained stoic. For a few seconds she thought that maybe she had presumed too much—perhaps stumbled into forbidden territory. But then his countenance cracked into a subtle but roguish smile, and he snatched the plate up, stepped back and waltzed off without another word.

13

Ian's words of support were still ringing in Quinn's ears when she pulled into her driveway at eight o'clock. She turned the engine off and sat in silence, staring at the door in front of her.

It's just a door.

Of course, it had just been a door the night before, when she walked in and found a corpse on the floor.

She hadn't anticipated feeling jumpy about going in alone tonight. Ian offered to follow her back and even check the house to make her feel better. But truly believing at the time that she would be fine, she declined.

Now she was second-guessing that decision.

Gathering her gumption and the doggie bag Ian prepared, she slid out of the truck and heard her name being called. Annalise Sardis, the renter of Number Five Bello Breakers, was standing in the drive of the yellow house, waving wildly.

"Quinn? Oh, Quinn! Have you got a second?"

The brunette woman was in her early fifties, and faring well with the passing years, although Quinn suspected she had countered the natural aging process with more than one visit to a plastic surgeon. She and her husband had made a killing in the cosmetics industry, then sold the business which bore their name, "Sardis Skincare." Now they spent most of their days vacationing in a variety of places they owned and rented, favoring warmth and the water from what Annalise told Quinn.

"Hi, Annalise," Quinn replied, mentally steeling herself as she crossed the cobblestone circle to where the woman stood by her Mercedes SUV. The Sardises were the opposite of the Garbers. Annalise and her husband were difficult, high-maintenance tenants, delivering nonsensical complaints by call or text almost every other day about some aspect of the property. The complaints included ridiculous grievances from "it's too sunny in the sun room" to "the woman staying in Number One walks past our house each morning around nine, interrupting our coffee time." Quinn expected this conversation would be no different.

"Everything all right?" Quinn asked.

"Well, no, Quinn, it's not. What happened last night?" Annalise's voice was sharp and demanding, her hands on her hips. "We were terrified! The police were banging on our door and asking us all kinds of questions—'Have we seen anyone in the area? Did we see anyone leave your house? Have we noticed anything strange? It just went on and on—"

"I'm sorry about that Annalise. I had a break-in. I was pretty unsettled by it all too."

"They said you thought there was a body," she said, abruptly switching to a hushed tone, "but that they didn't find one." She accentuated each of these last words, locking eyes with Quinn, her gaze begging for details.

Quinn's center hardened. "Did Shane...Deputy Cody tell you that?"

"I don't know which one it was. And then at the farmers market today the people at the honey stand were talking about it. Said you'd seen a corpse but when the police got there, it was gone."

Figures. There was an outdoor farmers and arts market on The Green every Saturday. The couple who ran the honey stand was notorious for spreading gossip about anyone and anything. Unfortunately, they had known Quinn since she was a girl and were well aware of her antics.

They probably ate this new information up like...well...honey, Quinn thought. "Uh, huh," she answered abruptly, refusing to bite on Annalise's bait.

"People were, um, saying that maybe...you'd..." Her sentence trailed off, one eyebrow rising hopefully.

Quinn's eyes narrowed. "Maybe I'd what?"

"That, you know, maybe you'd...imagined it."

Something snapped inside as Quinn's eyebrows shot toward the sky, along with her pitch. "Imagined a corpse on my floor? As in I saw something that wasn't there?" Quinn didn't care that Annalise was a client. She didn't care that there was another month left on their contract. Ire rose in her spirit like bitter bile and she stiffened. "That is ridiculous! You realize how ridiculous that sounds, right?"

"Well, I don't—" Annalise sputtered.

"That is cruel, unwarranted gossip and I don't appreciate it at all."

"Well, I'm not trying to be cruel—"

"Yes, my house was broken into last night, and yes, there was a body on the floor. And though you might not believe me, and this town might not believe me, I know what I saw and I am not going to give up until someone takes me seriously!" Quinn's chest heaved as she finished, her nerves blazing. Annalise's eyes were the size of yogurt lids, brimming equally with shock and offense.

"I...I..." Annalise stammered before recovering herself. "I

was not being cruel," she said indignantly. "I was only trying to find out if you were all right."

"Mm-hmm. Well, I'm fine. Thank you for your concern," Quinn said, and leaving the woman slack-jawed, turned and marched to her own back door.

Fuming, Quinn jammed her key in the lock, ready to be inside and out of Annalise's view, when she noticed a vase of flowers tucked beside the large urn to the left of the door.

"What in the world?" she said, and holding the doggie bag in one hand, lifted the arrangement of white roses, baby's breath, and blue hydrangea blooms with the other. Her name and address were scribbled on the attached envelope. Juggling both loads, she opened the door.

A wailing alarm immediately pierced her eardrums.

"Shoot!" Quinn bellowed. Racing to the alarm panel in the foyer, she set the flowers down and punched in the security code at the same time her cell phone rang.

It was the alarm monitoring company, calling in response to the triggered alarm. After assuring them all was well, she tossed the doggie bag in the fridge, and dropped onto a barstool, rubbing her hands over her face, her heart pounding. It had been so long since she used the alarm, she had unintentionally set it to go off immediately without any delay for deactivating it. She coughed as her heart uncomfortably skipped one beat, then another in the wake of the adrenaline rush. She breathed deeply from her belly, willing her pulse to slow.

As she vowed to set the alarm properly the next morning, her gaze fell across the flowers on the floor of the foyer. She retrieved them, grabbed the envelope and slid a finger beneath the flap, pulling the card out just enough to read the words, *Quinn, I still love you. Please—*

Embers of the anger smoldering after her altercation with Annalise flared as she jammed the card back inside the envelope. "You have got to be kidding me," she said caustically as she stomped to the trash can, dropped the arrangement in and slammed the lid shut.

After months of silence he has the nerve to make contact by sending flowers?

When she left Tampa, Simon had made it very, *very* clear he wanted nothing to do with her. Had he decided it was a mistake to let her go? Had he finally grasped what he had lost by not even trying to make it work? If so, he couldn't have chosen a more passive way to test the waters before taking a risk.

"Coward," Quinn grumbled, sparing one last loathsome glare for the few petals poking out from under the lid before turning away.

As her steps pounded toward the porch, it occurred to her that, actually, the gutless gesture made complete sense. Simon never had been one to stick his neck out. What's more, it showed just how little he understood her—to think that she would welcome this token attempt, or that it might open things back up between them.

The perfect ending to this day.

Flinging the French doors open with a gusto that sent them banging into the wall, she moved outside, the fresh air off the Gulf filling her lungs as she breathed in and out, then expelled a huge sigh. As she calmed down, her mind cleared, and eventually she felt a twinge of guilt.

I shouldn't have gotten so upset with Annalise.

Simon might have deserved her wrath, but Annalise hadn't. Not that she had been justified in prying the way she had, but unloading like that on the unsuspecting woman had been wrong. Annalise had simply been the pin that burst the balloon of all of Quinn's pent-up frustration over the events of the last twenty-four hours.

Once again, my short fuse gets me into trouble.

She would apologize first thing in the morning. Not only because it was the right thing to do, but also because they could lose a client over it. The last thing she needed was for Annalise to call the office and demand to speak to the owner—her dad. One, she didn't want her parents learning about the break-in that way and two, complaints like that were not going to boost her parents' fragile confidence in her, and she really needed them to believe in her right now.

The way that Ian believes in me.

Even in her own mind, the thought came off sounding a little bit needy. Sense told her she was grabbing onto this particular rope way too soon. But in her defense, at the moment it was the only one being thrown to her. If she wanted others to believe her—if she wanted Shane to believe her—she would need evidence. She would need to keep looking for something to support her story, as Ian suggested. Which was exactly what she was going to do.

Starting with the room where the body had been.

14

Every light in the kitchen and living room was on. With a flashlight in hand, Quinn's eyes raked over every surface, every corner, every nook and cranny, looking for anything that hinted something untoward happened there. She had already given it a once-over herself after the deputies left, even getting on her hands and knees to look along the cabinet baseboards and beneath furniture without any luck, but now it was time to dig deeper.

She walked the floor in a grid, shining the light ahead of her steps, looking for a mark, a smear, a foreign hair...but after pacing it twice, she still came up empty. She ran her hands over the cabinets and side tables in the living room not far from where the body had lain, checking for gashes or chipped wood, or maybe a speck of blood where his head might have struck a surface, ultimately sending him to the floor. Still nothing.

She felt along the countertops, swept the floor, looked in the shell-shaped urn she used as an umbrella stand in case something had fallen in it, even combed through the stack of mail on the counter—for what reason, she wasn't sure, other than it was somewhere else to look.

As a last resort, Quinn got down on the kitchen floor and lay flat on her stomach. Moving slowly, she spun in a circle on her belly, again shining the flashlight under everything—the refrigerator, the cabinets, the island, the sideboard chest—

Wait.

On the wall opposite the kitchen island, about six feet from where the body had lain, was a wooden sideboard chest painted a deep aquamarine. It was divided in half by two swinging doors and stretched almost all the way to the floor, where stubby, bulbous feet raised its base about an inch off the tile.

The gleam of the flashlight had illuminated something beneath the cabinet that was pressed up against its right rear foot. After hurriedly slipping on a dishwashing glove, Quinn moved around to the side of the chest, crouched down on the floor and shoved her hand under, her fingers scrabbling against the foot.

Yes!

Yanking her arm out, she sat up, revealing a plastic, cream-colored shirt button clutched in her fingers. Exactly the kind one might find on a men's button-down shirt.

And there it was. Proof she wasn't imagining things. That she hadn't made it up. Because three days ago she moved that cabinet away from the wall to paint. She had moved it to the other side of the room, swept the spot and even vacuumed to remove any possibility of dust or debris marring the new paint job. She had only just put the cabinet back on the afternoon of the break-in. So the button had to have ended up under it sometime after that. And she knew it hadn't come from her, because nothing she had worn in the last several days had this kind of button. The fact that it matched the color of the tile almost perfectly explained why neither she nor the deputies saw it during earlier searches.

Excitement coursed through Quinn, her nerve-endings

tingling with the anticipation of sharing this discovery. But the person filling her mind's eye wasn't Deputy Shane Cody.

It was Ian Wolfe.

Her nervous system did a one-eighty. A wash of apprehension flooded her as she thought of the handsome man at The Shed and his caring, determined expression as he listened to her, his strong hands wrapped around that mug, and the sincere concern in his tone when he insisted she use her alarm.

Oh, no.

Sitting on the cold tile, holding the button that was her only hope, Quinn realized that despite her best efforts to keep her distance from people and her resolution to swear off men for the foreseeable future, Ian Wolfe had managed to push past those self-imposed boundaries.

And she had absolutely no idea what to do about it.

15

Quinn had never found it easy to sit still for long. It was one reason she loved the kayak so much. You could paddle along or drift but you were always in motion, always headed somewhere. The steady current was dependable, forever working for you, never leaving you in the same stagnant place.

So it wasn't surprising she found it difficult to sit in a chair or pew or whatever for an extended length of time. This Sunday morning's service was proving no different, especially given last night's discovery and the way her mind was whirring with possibilities.

The sanctuary of Hope Community Church was bright and airy, with tall, stained-glass windows running down both sides. The coastal sun was bursting this morning, streaming in and splashing rainbows of color across the stark-white walls. The building had existed for decades, like something you would see on a postcard—complete with a cedar-shingled steeple atop a belfry pointing toward the heavens, contrasted by the white-washed exterior and wide front steps leading to towering double oak doors.

As usual, Quinn had taken her spot in the very back row. Across the aisle and a dozen rows up she could see Lena and her children, her friend listening intently to what Pastor James was sharing. Oddly enough his words coincided with yesterday's devotion, which Quinn hadn't gotten around to reading until this morning, after first calling Annalise to offer an apology the woman only half-heartedly accepted. The passage talked about how, once we've confessed something and repented, we've been forgiven and we shouldn't hold on to our guilt and keep revisiting it. Now Pastor James was asking a related question: how do you define yourself? It wasn't a question Quinn liked to ask. Lots of words like failure, liar, broken, disappointment, and loser came to mind. It wasn't a pleasant rumination for her. Even though she knew that wasn't how God defined her, it was sometimes hard to accept that He saw her as His child—forgiven, restored. So, before she knew it, she had let her mind drift like her kayak in the current of the Cove Springs River, carrying her along to last night at The Little Red Shed with its cozy string lights and jazz melodies...and Ian Wolfe.

Get a grip, Quinn, she thought, chastising herself. Again with Ian Wolfe? Why was he at the forefront of her mind? Why had he been able to push past all of the careful defenses she set up to ensure the emotional safety of herself and others?

Could it be that simply by believing in her, by giving her the benefit of the doubt without any strings attached or questionable glances, he had found a crack in her armor? She couldn't deny that it had been unbelievably satisfying to have someone side with her without having to convince them or work past ingrained biases. It had been a long time since that happened.

Simon had never been one to have her back like that. He had always questioned everything, always thought there was a better way.

Always.

The combination of intelligence, self-confidence and ambition that initially drew her to the fit, six-foot-three blonde with icy-blue eyes, eventually proved to be one of the very things that drove them apart.

Well, that and my substance abuse.

At the end Simon was right to question her, to second-guess her, because she was out of control. But when it all finally came out, when the episode in the courtroom led to the revelation of everything she had been hiding, he simply gave up. She remembered with an ache how he had put it so detachedly.

"I'm too smart, too ambitious and too busy to tie my life to someone with your issues. I'm a doctor for crying out loud. I can't be in a relationship with an addict. I love you, Quinn, I do, but love can't fix this. And I don't have it in me to sidetrack my life to try."

His words were cold and cruel and decisive, spoken on the evening of the courtroom incident while she was still in the hospital for observation. After her release the next day, she was only home half an hour before there was a knock on the door. It was a messenger service, there to collect the engagement ring Simon had slipped on her finger six months earlier over shrimp linguini at La Trattino, their favorite restaurant. She had ripped the pear-shaped two-carat stone off her finger, thrown it at the brown-uniformed messenger standing in the hallway, and slammed the door in his face.

It seems like a lifetime ago. I can't believe it's only been six months.

The sad truth was she didn't even really miss Simon, despite the fact that they had been together three years. Whatever they had when they started up must have died without either one of them noticing it, killed off slowly but surely by their respective long work hours and diverging paths, her poor choices and a relationship based on convenience more than commitment.

Quinn's cell vibrated silently in her purse. She dug it out and lifted it to read the text.

HOW ARE YOU?

Her heart dropped five stories. The text was from a number she didn't recognize, from an area code that did not belong to Seaglass Cove.

Who is this? she replied, her gut churning.

IAN

Instantly her dread evaporated. He had been thinking about her too. A warm buzz spread through her as her thumbs flew over her virtual keyboard.

I'm okay, thx, she typed. *How did you get my number?*

SMALL TOWN.

So? she fired back.

I ASKED AROUND.

Thought you didn't approve of gossip, she replied.

THIS WASN'T GOSSIP. THIS WAS FACT GATHERING.

She stifled a chuckle as she typed. *Ahh.*

SO WHERE ARE YOU? he asked.

I'm in church. Where are you? The responses which had been flying back to her like lightning halted. She wondered why while she waited for his reply, which came about half a minute later.

TALLAHASSEE. VISITING MY DAD IN HIS SENIOR HOME. MY BROTHER LIVES HERE. VISIT EVERY WEEK.

She felt a smile break over her face as affectionate admiration bubbled in her. This man cared about family, making the hour-long drive there and back to Tallahassee every Sunday for his dad. She liked that. A lot. Her parents were the two people who stuck by her through everything, no matter what, despite disappointment, fear, and just plain exhaustion. Family mattered to her. She was glad to find it mattered to Ian too.

Her stomach dipped slightly as it occurred to her that he hadn't mentioned last night that his dad and brother lived just an hour away. In fact, now that she thought about it, she realized she had done *all* the talking and hadn't asked a single real question about him. Nothing about his family. Nothing about his life before Seaglass Cove, or how he ended up here. She would have to change that. Inspiration struck and she sent out, *When will you be back?*

NOT TILL TONIGHT. AROUND 5.

Quinn held her breath for a moment as an idea came to her. Should she? After all, the suggestion wouldn't be completely off-the-wall. She did have news to tell him. Her thumbs flew again. *Got plans?*

JUST ME AND THE TV.

Come over to my place instead. I've got news, she baited.

??? WHAT?

You'll have to wait. Rather tell you in person.

YOU'RE KILLING ME, he replied.

This time she did chuckle. *Sorry. In person.*

ADDRESS?

She gave it to him, told him it was her turn to feed him, and not to eat before he came over. He promised he wouldn't. It looked like she was going to finally have to make that trip to the grocery store after all.

But not before she made a couple of other stops first.

16

The day was gorgeous, a canvas of cheerful blue skies painted with puffy white clouds and the sweet smell of blooming wildflowers caught up in the breeze as Quinn pulled out of the church parking lot with a plan.

It was a perfect day to be on the water and she couldn't wait to put her kayak into the Cove Springs River and follow it for miles, just her and the water. Even the thought of it slowed her heartbeat and deepened her breathing, which was a good thing. What she was planning on doing after the kayak excursion would definitely have the opposite effect. Shane came on duty at three o'clock, and if she timed it right, she could be at the sheriff's department before he left for patrol and could confront him in person about the button.

"Confront" is the wrong word, Quinn.

Okay, so she would *show* him the button. Prove that she wasn't imagining things. He might still argue the guy hadn't been dead, but he wouldn't be able to say that she imagined him. It would at least be a step in the right direction.

A check of the dashboard clock said it was twelve fifteen,

which gave her a little over two hours. She had already changed in the bathroom at church so she wouldn't have to go back home. A quick trip through the drive-thru of The Chick'n Salad Hut for a sandwich and a side of fruit made lunch easy, and she gobbled it down on the drive to the river. Once in the parking lot of the launch point, she only had to register with the excursion service for a return shuttle pickup at two fifteen before she was carting her kayak to the water.

As soon as she slipped the craft into the gentle, crystal-clear river, an intense peace washed over her, her mind truly clear for the first time in days. Her teal hull skimmed soundlessly through the water as she paddled rhythmically on one side, then the other. This section was shallow and thick with eel grass that lined the banks and swayed beneath the surface in the mild current, like performers in a synchronized routine with flashes of mullet darting in and out for added show.

She dragged her fingertips in the water, which remained at seventy-two degrees year-round, thanks to the deep underground springs that fed it. Gripping the paddle again, she sped on, passing banks dotted with palmettos and the white, fragrant blooms of spider lilies. Two turtles sunbathed on a fallen log, while a red-shouldered hawk soared above her, its wings outstretched, rising and falling on a draft.

The river wasn't crowded today, which was surprising given the good weather and the fact that locals liked to squeeze in as many trips as possible before the touristy months. There were only a half dozen other paddlers within sight, and eventually they would spread out too, as each adopted their own pace. As for Quinn, she was only going three miles and had an hour and a half to do it, so she wasn't in a hurry.

After about twenty minutes, the river transitioned, widening where several live oaks towered over the banks' edges. The river bottom became less marshy green, as the eel grass tapered off until there was nothing but water, transparent to the bottom. In the varying sunlight and depths it appeared as shades of brilliant turquoise, white, sand, or all three at once, like a geode rock cut clean through and laid bare.

The waterway began to wind here, snaking back and forth under shady, overhead growth, creating a tunnel-like feel and decreasing visibility downriver. Most of the paddlers had passed her by this time, leaving only one within view behind her. She was almost alone on the water. Exactly how she liked it. Especially as she neared her favorite section.

She felt a smile break on her face as she spotted a trio of manatees in the water ahead, their massive forms fully visible in the glassy river. "Hello, beauties," she whispered as she passed where they were lolling, six feet or so from her kayak. Unable to withstand colder sea temperatures during winter months, these giant, lumbering sea cows often sought out the consistent warmth of the underground spring-fed river, even at this time of year. Sometimes they followed it all the way to the head, several miles further inland. On another day she might slow to stay with them, see if they might approach her, as they were sometimes known to do. But there wasn't time today and she gently dipped her oar in once more, the largest of the manatees turning toward her as she left them behind, almost as if bidding her farewell.

As she swiveled to watch them, she caught a glimpse of the kayaker behind her, his orange, rented craft a vibrant contrast to the blue-green waters. He seemed to barely spare the creatures a glance before pressing on, paddling more aggressively than Quinn would have advised in the vicinity of the manatees.

Must have a tight schedule, she thought, wondering if maybe he hadn't allowed enough time to meet his return shuttle. But thoughts of him quickly left her as thirty yards ahead the entrance to the Magic Forest came into view.

She had dubbed this section by that name when she was eight years old, when her father used to take her on trips in a tandem kayak down this very river. More than twenty years later she still believed the name was well-deserved. The beginning of the passage was marked by a grouping of enormous bald cypress trees she had always thought of as the gatekeepers to this realm. These giants shot a hundred feet into the air from bases as wide as cars, the roots visible above the waterline like impossibly thick fingers digging for something on the river bottom. Once inside, more bald cypress trees dotted the narrowing river, their overhanging limbs creating a canopy of tightly compacted needles draped with curtains of ash-grey Spanish moss. The current picked up a bit, and Quinn's spirits lifted as she worked to navigate the labyrinth, dodging trees and fallen trunks before the current slowed again. Here she let herself drift, mindlessly eyeing the gorgeous scenery as she pondered Ian Wolfe.

She had asked him to dinner. Sure, there was the button and all that, but there was no avoiding the reality that she had, in fact, asked him over for dinner.

Did I make a mistake?

Her failed relationship with Simon had left scars and now was fostering doubts. The echoes of the labels she often applied to herself reverberated in her mind. Would Ian even want to be with someone like her? But then, she had told him her stories and apparently he hadn't been scared off. To the contrary, he was the one who reached out to *her* this morning. And he just agreed to what could conceivably be considered a dinner date. Or in his mind was it just a meeting with a new friend, with the goal of digging through a mystery together?

Which was it?

A sinking feeling curdled in the pit of her stomach. *Was that all it was? Just a friend helping a friend?*

Quinn breathed deeply, inhaling the musty scent of Spanish moss as somewhere to her left a bird called out, clicking and cawing. Her insides hummed at the realization that she was definitely interested in this being more than an opportunity to relay developments in the burglary situation.

The real question, then, was what was Ian thinking?

She remembered Meghan Carne and the way Ian had interacted with her at The Shed. A knot of disappointment tightened in her chest, as the memory left her fairly certain that, for Ian, dinner tonight was likely just two friends hashing through a puzzle.

But maybe that wasn't so bad. She needed more friends in this town. People who truly had her back, and especially ones untainted by her history. Plus, romance invited drama, something she definitely didn't need. In the end, "just friends" might be for the best all the way around.

QUINN ARRIVED at the take-out point at exactly 2:13 p.m., leaving just a couple of minutes to spare before the shuttle was scheduled to leave. With the use of a cart, she towed her kayak to the shuttle van, where the driver helped her load it onto the trailer hitched to its rear. She was climbing in the van when she noticed that the kayaker who stayed with her for most of the journey was loading his rental kayak onto a cart at the water's edge. The driver was hustling to meet him.

For the briefest of moments, the man's eyes flashed to meet Quinn's and a warning chill cut through her. Then he looked away and went back to fiddling with the kayak's straps again. Her senses on high-alert, she climbed the rest of the way inside the van and slid over as far as possible on the first row until she was directly behind the driver's seat. She watched as the man and the driver noisily dragged the cart through the gravel lot, unable to pinpoint exactly why she had been so triggered by his gaze. But she couldn't shake the feeling that something about it just felt *off*.

They rolled the cart past the van to the trailer at the back, the man not sparing her a single glance. When they passed from view, Quinn faced forward, replaying the kayak trip in her mind, especially the fact that he had stayed with her the whole time even though her pace had been rather slow. Other kayakers had caught up to her and passed by, but not him.

But if they were on the same shuttle, his proximity was probably a harmless coincidence.

Or not.

Contempt welled in her. She despised this paranoia or whatever it was rearing its head again. Finding freedom from that feeling was one of the best parts of going through her rehabilitation program—coming out of the neurotic haze she had inflicted upon herself with her bad choices and self-medication. Now it was back. Only she wasn't *on* anything.

The banging at the back of the truck from the loading of the kayak ceased, and Quinn steeled herself, expecting the man to hop into the van with her.

Hopefully he'll keep moving to one of the other rows.

But when he didn't climb in, she swiveled around to see him walking away from the trailer toward the back of the parking lot. Relief washed over her, and feeling a bit ridiculous for overreacting, she turned as the driver appeared at the door.

"Looks like it's just you this run," he said. "You good?"

"Yep," Quinn replied, grateful they didn't need to wait on a straggling kayaker, which happened sometimes. She really needed to get to the sheriff's department by two forty-five.

As the engine started up, Quinn's thoughts turned to meeting with Shane and she began running through exactly what she was going to say. The van circled around to the exit, giving her a direct view of the rear of the lot. What she saw made her heart freeze.

The kayaker was sitting in the passenger seat of a car parked in the last row—a grey Sonata driven by a man wearing sunglasses and a baseball cap.

17

"I don't get it," Quinn said, pointing at the button inside the clear baggie now held by Shane. "Why won't you believe me?"

They sat across the table from each other in the drab eight-by-eight interview room Shane had taken her to. "Look, Quinn, it's not a matter of believing you. It's just that this button doesn't prove anything. It could have come from anywhere. Could be your dad's or from somebody who rented the place years ago before your parents moved in." His voice was firm, his face tight with frustration.

"No, it couldn't be," Quinn said. Her words were sharp despite the fact that she had promised herself she would remain calm no matter what. But she was finding that harder than anticipated because he had barely let her get her story out before dismissing it wholeheartedly. Her eyes flicked to the mirror on the wall across from her, which was clearly an observation window.

The whole department is probably watching on the other side—gathered to hear the crazy woman roll out her latest tale. "I told you," she said, shoving aside those thoughts. "I cleaned that entire area just days ago. No one else has been in the house since then but me, you, your guys and whoever broke in." She waved a hand at the baggie. "It even looks like the kind of button that would be on the shirt he was wearing. The only explanation is that it came from him, because the buttons on your uniforms don't match," she said, that fact obvious given the black buttons on the shirt he was wearing.

"No, that's the only explanation you're willing to accept," Shane retorted, his voice rising slightly in volume, "because you're determined to stick with this story about a corpse. But Quinn, nothing supports it and this," he flipped the plastic bag onto the table so that it slid a little, stopping in front of her, "means nothing. It could be *your* button for all we know. I mean, did you check that?"

His tone was infuriating. Heat crept up in her center, like the slow rise of mercury in a thermometer. "I haven't worn anything with a button like that, and you're not even considering the whole situation with the guy I saw in the car watching me...following me! Twice!"

"What, the guy in a grey sedan? Like a million other grey sedans out there? The guy—"

"Not just a grey sedan. A grey Sonata. With the same driver—"

"But you can't be sure it was the same person. Or even the same Sonata."

She pressed her lips together so tightly that she could feel them pucker. "Well, I didn't get the license plate, if that's what you mean—"

Shane shook his head. "Quinn, I'll bet if you went outside now, you wouldn't have to wait five minutes before a couple of Sonatas, grey ones even, passed by. You know how many tourists we get here, driving in from Tallahassee. Rental car companies rent grey sedans out in droves. Lots of Sonatas. And some guy wearing a ball cap? Come on."

This is pointless. He's never going to take me seriously unless I drag an actual body in here. "I think that maybe I need to talk to your supervisor, Shane. Because it's clear that you have a blind spot when it comes to me and this situation."

"I've already spoken to my supervisor." His tone was flat, but his expression smacked of satisfaction.

"What?"

"When you called me on the way over and told me what you had," he inclined his head toward the button, "I thought I should let him know, and he agrees with me. You need to calm down and let us do our job. Eventually the guy that broke in will slip up and we'll catch him and you'll see that he wasn't dead and this isn't some big conspiracy. No one is following you. No one is out to get you." He squinted at her appraisingly. "I have to ask. You're not..." He let the end of the sentence trail off, as if she was supposed to catch his meaning without forcing him to verbalize the entire question.

She did catch his meaning and anger flashed through her. "What? Self-medicating again? Drinking again? No, Shane, I'm not," she said, clenching her teeth.

"It's just, this sounds a lot like Tampa."

"It's not at all like Tampa. But thanks for your concern." She glared at the mirror. "And you can tell your supervisor the same. It's time for your shift. I'm gonna get out of your hair." She shot up out of her chair and he followed suit, walking behind her as she flung open the door and marched back down the hallway toward the lobby.

She was just reaching for the handle to the exit into the lobby when the sound of heavy footsteps lumbering toward them drew her attention. Another deputy was hustling down the hallway. He caught up to them and leaned over, whispering something to Shane. When he finished, the deputy briefly cast a dubious look in Quinn's direction then went back the way he came.

Shane held Quinn's gaze, his features like stone, even harder than before if that were possible.

"What? What is it?" Quinn asked.

"First call of my shift just came in. There's been some trouble."

"Okay. So why are you looking at me like that?"

"Because apparently *you're* the troublemaker."

"I want her arrested!" Annalise Sardis bellowed, pointing a French-manicured finger at Quinn.

Quinn, Annalise and Shane stood in the driveway of Number Five Bello Breakers, gathered around the driver's side of Annalise's Mercedes SUV. Mr. Sardis, exceedingly tanned and dressed in navy shorts and a white golf shirt, stood several feet behind them under the rear entrance portico, choosing at least for the moment to stay out of it. Based on Quinn's experience with the couple, this was how it usually went, and honestly, Annalise didn't need any help. She was capable of raising plenty of stink all by herself.

"Look at that! Just look at it!" Annalise swung her arm around like a sprinkler head so that it was pointed at the car. "What am I supposed to do about *that!*"

Spray-painted across the pristine ebony exterior of the Mercedes Benz in huge, traffic-cone-orange letters were the words:

MIND YOUR OWN BUSINESS

"It's awful, Annalise," Quinn began, "but I don't know—"

"What do you mean 'I don't know'? This was *you*. First you berate me in public, insulting me at the top of your lungs, calling me a 'gossip'—"

Quinn's mouth dropped. "Now wait a minute—I did not berate you in public."

"You stood right here last night and when I asked you how you were doing after the break-in, *out of concern*," she spat, emphasizing the last words as she swiveled her head to Shane then back to Quinn, "you laid into me like a crazy person—"

Indignation flooded Quinn. "Now hold on, Annalise, I was not acting like a 'crazy person' and I did not do this to your car!"

Shane held his palms out at both of them. "Okay, okay, just stop for a minute," he said forcefully, his volume just shy of a bark. "Mrs. Sardis, is your argument with Quinn yesterday the only reason you think she did this? Do you have any evidence it was her? Did you see her—"

"See her? I heard her. She told me basically to mind my own business yesterday and now," she dragged a hand through the air across the vehicle, like a game show hostess heralding a prize, "the same thing is painted all over it. Thousands of dollars of damage. Thousands!"

"What about you, Mr. Sardis?" Shane asked, turning to eye Annalise's husband.

"He didn't see anything, either," Annalise replied for him, "And he wasn't here when she lashed out at me." Mr. Sardis kept quiet, but nodded in agreement.

It was clear to Quinn that she was not going to sway Annalise so she directed herself to Shane. "Shane, please, come on. You can't possibly think I'd do something like this."

But instead of reassuring her with words, or even a subtle glance, he asked, "So you deny having anything to do with it?"

Quinn's mouth dropped in sheer incredulity. "Of course I do!"

This was beyond unbelievable. Hopelessness hit Quinn hard as she realized exactly how little Shane must think of her if he was actually entertaining the notion that she could have done this. It wouldn't be long before word of this incident would leak out too, and she would be tried and convicted in the court of public opinion once more. *How long before it filters into the Hope Center, to church, to the shops on the Green, Miguel...*

She realized Shane was speaking to Annalise and tuned back in to their conversation. "...I can make a report and take your statement, and of course, we'll investigate, but I doubt much will come of it. Has there been anyone you've had a run-in with lately or trouble—"

"You mean besides her?" Annalise interrupted drolly.

"Yes, besides her," Shane said.

"No. No one," Annalise answered, glowering at Quinn.

"Well, then let me get some information from you," Shane replied, stepping toward his patrol vehicle, "so we can fill out an incident report."

From behind them on the circle came the sound of another vehicle approaching. Quinn turned to see Ian Wolfe pulling up in her driveway in a black Jeep Cherokee.

Another pang of failure struck Quinn as she pulled her phone out.

4:15.

In the aftermath of Annalise's vandalism report, Quinn had completely forgotten that Ian was coming over. And that she was supposed to make him dinner. Though it was not yet five o'clock, and he was definitely early, there was no way she could manage it now.

She wanted to find a rock and crawl under it as Ian approached, his face scrunched in consternation. "What's going on?" he said, his gaze moving from Quinn to Annalise, the ruined Mercedes and Shane, then finally to Mr. Sardis on the portico, his arms folded across his chest.

Quinn pulled Ian aside and laid out the basics for him while Shane took Annalise's statement. After she had filled him in, Ian approached Shane and Annalise. "Excuse me for interrupting. I'm Ian Wolfe," he said.

"The Little Red Shed, yeah, I know," replied Shane.

"Ms. Bello's given me the rundown of what's going on. I wanted to ask if you needed her for this or if she's free to go?"

Shane lowered the clipboard, his shoulders straightening as he turned toward Ian. "Well, she's not a witness. But she has been accused by Mrs. Sardis of being involved, so I'll want to take a statement."

"Now?"

"Well, not until I finish up with Mrs. Sardis and take some photos."

"Then would it be all right if we went next door? Ms. Bello has a prior engagement and you may be awhile with the...Mrs. Sardis." Annalise's face was twisted in a scowl, her eyes barely slits as she glared at Ian. Apparently she didn't appreciate him coming to Quinn's aid. "We'll be right next door," Ian said, thumbing at Number Four, "whenever you're ready to talk to her."

"What are you, her lawyer?" Shane asked, a note of derision in his tone.

"Just a concerned friend. So we'll see you in a bit then?"

Shane paused momentarily before nodding, then turned his back to them and continued taking Annalise's statement.

18

"I don't know what to say," Quinn remarked as she led Ian inside. She dropped her purse in the foyer and moved through to the kitchen where she turned, leaning against the counter. "Thank you for getting me out of there."

"No problem," Ian said, gesturing to one of the bar stools.

"Yeah, of course. Sit," she told him, then felt her face flush as a fresh wave of sickening remembrance struck. "Dinner! I was supposed to make you dinner—"

"I'm early," he said, waving her off. "It's not your fault."

"But you're not *that* early. And the groceries! I never even made it to the store. I was going to. I was going straight there after the sheriff's department but then Shane got the call about Annalise's car—"

"Hey, slow down," Ian said, motioning with both hands for her to put on the brakes. "It's all good. You don't have to feed me." He hopped off the stool and pointed to it. "How about you sit instead while I check things out," he suggested, rising and nodding at the fridge.

She reluctantly took his place on the stool, as he walked over to the refrigerator. He swung the stainless steel door open, revealing bottles of water, milk, a gallon of sweet tea, a carton of eggs, assorted cheeses in the deli drawer and not much else. With one arm still hanging on the door, he dramatically swiveled his head back toward her. "This is pretty pathetic. No wonder you're always eating at The Shed."

"Yeah, well," she said, tipping her head in acknowledgment, her ponytail swinging. "I never claimed to be Rachael Ray."

"And here I was thinking *I* was the reason you were coming into The Shed so much. But it turns out you're just a lazy cook." His grey eyes shimmered teasingly as a nervous flutter rippled down Quinn's back.

He pulled out a bottle of water and plunked it on the counter in front of her. "Drink. It'll help."

"Thanks," she said. And he was right. The chilled water trickled down her throat to her center, refreshing and reviving her.

His gaze passed over the trash can tucked beside the aquamarine sideboard chest. Its hinged lid was still propped open by the smashed flower arrangement, a few damaged white rose and blue hydrangea petals poking out. Ian inclined his head toward it. "What's going on there?"

"Ugh," Quinn answered, letting out a hiss of breath. "It's from my ex. His idea of reestablishing contact."

"Not well received, I take it?"

"Let's just say that if I had to choose between coming home to Simon or another intruder in my house, I'd probably pick the intruder."

"Yikes," Ian replied, then flicked a forefinger in the direction of Number Five. "So Shane—he's not taking her seriously, is he? He doesn't really think you would vandalize that car?"

She ran her thumb over the water bottle's label, her mouth turning down. "You know, I actually think he might."

"That's nuts."

"Yeah, well, I'm beginning to think he thinks *I'm* nuts. And apparently his supervisor agrees."

Ian's forehead wrinkled. "What are you talking about?"

She motioned for him to follow her to the couch where she plunged into the whole story, including finding the button and the man she thought had been watching her earlier that day at the river take-out point.

"The button is at the sheriff's department but I took a photo," she said, slipping her phone out to show him. "See?" she asked as Ian studied it. "It's exactly the kind that would've been on the sort of shirt he was wearing. It's too bad I didn't get a photo of the body on my floor," she said self-deprecatingly, as he handed the phone back.

"Well, you weren't exactly thinking about documenting evidence when you found him. And you had no idea who else was in here. It would've been dangerous to stick around and snap photos. You made the right decision."

It was a small thing, his affirmation that she had done the right thing that night. But it was nice to hear someone say it all the same. "Thank you," she said.

He watched her, the corner of his mouth pulling up into a thoughtful smile. "I was really glad you asked me over tonight."

"You were?"

"Mm-huh," he nodded. "I wanted to check on you anyway. You still seemed a little out of sorts when you left last night."

"Oh. Well—"

A loud banging on the back door interrupted her.

"That'll be Barney Fife," Ian said, forcing a laugh from Quinn. "Why don't you finish up with him as quickly as you can while I worry about finding us something to eat. You can tell me the rest when I get back."

Quinn's spine went rigid. "What? No, this was my idea. I was going to cook for you."

"Well, unless you were planning on eggs with a side of eggs, someone's going to have to run out." There was another, more impatient knock on the door.

"Fine," she said, sighing dramatically, both of them rising off the couch and walking to the foyer. As she stretched her hand out to turn the lock on the door, she sensed that he was close, maybe just a few feet behind her.

"You can cook next time," he said, his words soft-spoken but confident.

For just a moment she froze with her fingers on the lock, grateful that he couldn't see the grin stretched across her face.

IT FELT ODD, being alone with Shane as they sat down in the living room so she could answer his questions. She couldn't stop replaying mental images from two nights ago, and thinking about how unsuccessful that exchange had been. She had a bad feeling this wasn't going to go any better. She took the couch while he took the overstuffed chair across from her, peppering her with questions immediately.

Where had she been earlier in the day?

Had she seen anyone on the Sardises' property? What about near the Mercedes?

Had she seen anyone in the neighborhood or on the board-walk behind the homes?

Could she think of anyone who might have a reason to vandalize the Sardises' property or who might have an issue with them?

And his final, insulting question: Did she have anything to do with it?

Although frustration roiled in her belly, Quinn worked hard to be cooperative and pleasant, at least as much as was possible when she suspected that, on some level, Shane believed she might be guilty. Finally he handed her the clipboard to sign her statement. She glanced it over, looked up and dropped it onto her lap with a thump. "Look, Shane, I know you've got your doubts about me, but you don't seriously think I would do something like this do you?"

He sighed. "Just sign it, Quinn. Okay?"

Shaking her head, she scribbled her name on the bottom and handed it back. He took it and set it beside him, then looked at her with distinct sadness in his expression. The sudden change was unnerving and she tried to ready herself for whatever was coming next.

"Quinn, have you been drinking?"

The question stunned her, and ribbons of cold threaded through her chest. "What? Why would you ask me that? I am one hundred percent sober! You are way out of line with this, Shane. This is—"

"I found an empty vodka bottle in your garbage can on the street."

The cold spread, frost now filling her veins. "Wait...what? No, you didn't. I didn't put a vodka bottle in my garbage. I don't *have* a bottle of vodka."

"Well it's in there."

"Then someone else put it there because it isn't mine." Her bones seemed to be vibrating and a humming filled her head as her heart skipped a beat. Her hand moved to her chest, pressing on it, as if that would alter the pattern. "I dragged it out there this morning. It's been there all day. Anyone could have thrown that bottle in."

She wanted to rail at him for digging through her trash, for invading her privacy, but as a lawyer she knew that once she rolled the trash receptacle onto the street—onto city property for collection—she waived any right to privacy she might have otherwise had in its contents. "Where's the bottle? I want to see it."

"In my patrol car. Along with the can of orange spray paint I found in there with it."

Quinn actually guffawed at that news. "You found what?"

"One can of orange spray paint. It matches the paint on the SUV."

"Of course it does." Quinn rocketed from her seat and walked toward the porch, staring out the glass doors to the sea beyond. The sun was low in the sky, sending brilliant color across the edges of the horizon and shimmering reflections off the rolling waters. She put her hands on her hips and continued talking without looking at him.

"Do you really think that if I did that I'd be stupid enough to put the evidence in my own trash can?"

"I don't know what you might do after a few drinks."

She spun around, her shoulders quivering. This was unbelievable. It couldn't be happening. Not here. Not now. Not when she was just starting over and getting a handle on things. "I think you should go."

He stood, his face solemn. "Are we gonna find your fingerprints on that can?"

"Not unless someone put them there, which honestly, at this point, I'm starting to think someone out there might do—"

"You realize it's nearly impossible to plant fingerprints, right, Quinn? You being an attorney and all, I figured you'd know that." The caustic sarcasm dripping from his words sent a flash of heat through Quinn that drove her frustration to the boiling point as he continued talking. "So if they're on there—"

"I know you still hold Annie against me, Shane," she snapped, feeling a rush as she let her anger loose, "and I'll be forever sorry about that. I'm still crushed about what happened to her, but—"

Shane's face flushed red. "Hold on a minute. That has nothing to do with this."

"Really?" she countered, her pitch rising. "Because it seems to me it has everything to do with you refusing to even *consider* that I might be telling the truth about all this crazy stuff that's happening to me. You've turned your whole department against me and who knows who else in this town—"

"I haven't turned anyone against you! And my take on this and on you has everything to do with the fact that you have a history as a liar and a drinker and a self-medicator who not six months ago was so hopped-up that you nearly shot someone in a courtroom—"

"Get. Out." The words seethed from between Quinn's gritted teeth.

"I'm not—"

"Deputy, I think it's time that you leave." Ian's deep voice boomed from the foyer, where he stood just inside the door, a bulky white plastic bag suspended from his hand, resting against his thigh. "Unless you're planning on arresting Ms. Bello, it seems to me you're done here." Though his tone was calm, his stance was all business—feet spread shoulder-width apart, shoulders back, jaw jutted.

Shane's gaze flashed from Ian to Quinn and without another word, he marched to the foyer, sidestepped Ian and walked out, slamming the door behind him.

Ian's eyes widened as he stood his ground. "Um, did I miss something?"

"A lot. How much did you hear?"

"I walked in on you yelling at him for not taking your story seriously."

Embarrassment surged through her as her shoulders sank. "I was trying so hard to keep my cool."

"You were pretty fiery."

"Comes with the red hair, unfortunately," she said sheepishly.

"Well, from what I heard it sounded like he deserved it. He

was out of line. Completely unprofessional. You're not wrong about him having a personal bias."

She was about to thank him for stepping in and keeping her from saying something to Shane that she would have regretted, when she noticed the all-too-familiar bag in his hand. Amusement drove one corner of her mouth up. "What's that?"

"Oh, yeah," he said, looking down at the bag like he had forgotten he was holding it. "I grabbed take-out from a food truck on The Green. Pepe's? Ever tried it? It's pretty good."

A smile split her face. "Sounds perfect."

19

The wind was gentle and cool, blowing off the Gulf and across Quinn's skin. She and Ian sat at the bronzed dining table on her back porch finishing the last of dinner. Sea gulls squawked contentiously down on the beach, fighting over something in the sand, while a couple walked past them pointing at the birds and laughing.

Ian had opted for chicken burritos with red and green peppers, onions and cheese, chips with guac and tomatillo sauce for dipping, and sopapillas with honey for dessert. She didn't have the heart to tell him about her regular patronage of Pepe's, but just as she was polishing off the last bite of burrito, she slipped and mentioned that the dish was one of her favorites and the whole truth came out.

"I can't believe you didn't say anything," he said, leaning back from the table, looking defeated. "I could have gone back out for something else."

"Don't be ridiculous. This is great. There's a reason why I eat there almost every night."

"Other than the fact that you're too lazy to go to the grocery store?" he said wryly, one eyebrow peaking jauntily.

"Lazy's a strong word," she said, dipping a chip in the guac then pointing it at him. "It's more like selective disinclination."

"Throwing a big word at it doesn't change the fact that you're a grown woman who doesn't seem to be able to feed herself."

"Are you saying you want me to stop coming into The Shed for my meals?"

He narrowed his eyes playfully. "Um, no. That is absolutely *not* what I'm saying."

"Good," she said, and in return Ian unleashed a brilliant smile that emphasized his pronounced cheekbones.

He tilted his head toward his shoulder, casting a sidelong glance at his phone on the table. "So we've actually gone past our twenty-minute moratorium on talking about what just happened. You ready to spill it?"

Before starting dinner, she asked if they could have twenty minutes without talking about Shane or what just happened, or any of it, so she could clear her head. He agreed and they instead engaged in a back and forth about favorite music—hers, Panic! at the Disco, his, U2—favorite movies—hers, the Keira Knightley version of *Pride and Prejudice*, his, *The Hurt Locker*—food—both Mexican, and so on. Then they discussed the seafood festival scheduled in Seaglass Cove for later that month and how crazy things would get with the tourists after that. But he was right, the twenty minutes had long passed and she was ready to give him all the gory details anyway.

She picked up where she left off earlier, explaining Shane's disappointing reaction to the button at the sheriff's department and the call that brought them to Annalise. "...And that's when you showed up in the driveway. Then, after you left to get dinner, Shane launched into me..."

Quinn summarized giving her statement to Shane and the revelations he made about the vodka bottle and the spray can, as well as his not-so-veiled accusations. "And that's pretty much when I lost it."

"I wouldn't say you *lost* it, exactly."

"Well, I wasn't exactly holding it in." She could tell Ian was fighting the urge to smile.

"And this—Annalise—really thinks you did it?"

"Oh, she *definitely* thinks I did it. And Shane probably does too after finding that stuff in the trash can."

"Why would you be stupid enough to dump the evidence in your own trash can?"

She shrugged. "Exactly what I said." She took a sip of iced tea, set her glass down and ran her finger around it, catching the beads of sweat dripping down the side. "You know, you've asked a lot of questions about me, but I realized this morning that I didn't really ask anything about you last night."

"Hmm."

"Yeah, hmm," she echoed. "So was that just me being rude or were you intentionally steering the conversation away from yourself?"

"Oh, definitely you being rude," he spouted, winking at her as he picked up his own glass, chugged back a piece of ice and chewed it.

The beach took on a different quality as six o'clock approached, a tranquil beauty settling over it as the bold heat of day eased into a mellow warmth. The angle and hue of light also shifted into something softer, accompanied by silver clouds hovering low on the horizon where they met the deep, dark blue. The two shared a quiet moment, both gazing out toward the water, until Quinn glanced sideways at him while his focus was still on the shoreline.

The golden late afternoon rays revealed random blonde strands in his light-brown hair, fairer flecks of grey that were almost blue in his dark irises, and the occasional freckle along his forearms. He could have been anywhere, with anyone and he was choosing to be here with her, even with all the craziness surrounding her.

Why?

"I need to ask you something," she said, breaking the silence and fidgeting in her seat.

He eyed her quizzically. "Okay."

"After everything I've told you—especially after what Shane found in my trash can—you still believe me. Even though I'm basically a stranger. Trouble clearly follows me around, and yet, you're still here. I don't get it."

"Well, first of all, you're not a stranger. We've shared guacamole and that, my friend, means we have now crossed over from mere acquaintances into something altogether different. And second, like I said, I believe in second chances. And third, I also believe you're not an idiot. And only an idiot would have tossed that junk into her own trash."

"Even if I was drinking?"

"You aren't drinking." He said it like it was a statement of fact, leaving no room whatsoever in his tone for any degree of doubt. She could have hugged him.

"You seem awfully sure."

"I'm a good judge of character," he said, his gaze boring into her.

"Okay. Well, then, *friend*, I want to know more about you."

"Like what?"

"For starters, how did you end up down here?"

He clasped his hands in his lap. "Like I said, my dad lives in Tallahassee, and so does my brother. So it just made sense to move nearby. Dad wasn't doing so great and I wanted to be able to help."

"Where were you before you moved here?"

"Born and bred in Chicago. Dad and Mom moved down here to escape the cold years ago, and then she passed. My brother followed them, but when we had to put Dad in an assisted living facility, it just seemed right for me to make a change."

"Your dad—I mean, given your age—he has to be kind of young for an assisted living facility, doesn't he?" Ian couldn't have been older than his late thirties, and that was pushing it.

"Ahh. Yeah, well, I am just thirty-five but they had me really late. I was a surprise when mom was forty-three. Dad was forty-seven."

"Oh, wow."

He laughed. "That was my dad's reaction, or so I'm told. My brother's fifty-two. We aren't that close, but I was kind of hoping that would change once I moved down here."

"And how did The Little Red Shed come about? I love the pun by the way. Little Red...Wolfe. Funny."

He chuckled. "Yeah. Not everybody gets that. But I liked it—I mean, the place was already painted red so it just sort of named itself."

"How did you find it?"

"I was driving down the coast checking out the different communities, seeing where I might land, and there it was. Abandoned, in need of a little love, just waiting for someone to make it into something more. I guess, at the time, that sort of spoke to me."

"Did you have a place like it in Chicago?"

Tension seemed to draw his body taut. "No. I was doing something else."

"Let me guess," she said.

He smiled. "Give it your best shot."

"Okay, but if I get it right on the first try, *I* get the last sopapilla," she said, shaking the container that held the last of the deep-fried, donut-like confections powdered with sugar.

He nodded approvingly. "Fair enough."

She didn't hesitate. "You were a cop."

Surprise stretched Ian's features as he let out an exaggerated whoosh of air. He leaned on the table, his muscled fore-arms crossed in front of him. "How in the world did you guess that?"

So she had been right. She couldn't keep the hint of a smug smile from creeping onto her face. "As an attorney I came across a lot of police officers. You learn the tells."

She nodded toward the front door. "The way you were standing there when you told Shane to leave...there was something about your stance that seemed military-like. And you spoke to him with the kind of confidence that a person has with an equal. I might have guessed you were in the military except you just told me you moved from Chicago, "born and bred," and it sounded like you'd never left. So cop seemed more likely. And then there's the way you were asking me questions last night. Like you were conducting an interview. I realized later that during our entire conversation I never asked you anything about yourself. You kept the focus on me, and did it so well that I didn't even notice. So, my guess...cop." The wind picked up, blowing a swath of red hair that had fallen out of her ponytail across her face. She brushed it back, tucking it behind her ear.

"Not bad, Detective Bello. Which, by the way, was your only slip-up. I was a cop, but by the time I left the job, it was Detective Wolfe, not Officer Wolfe."

Quinn snapped her fingers in front of her. "Shucks. Well, it's close enough—"

"I don't think so," Ian said, as their hands shot out for the sopapilla simultaneously. When they each grasped an opposite corner, their eyes flashed to the other's and with matching grins, they yanked hard on the fried pastry so that it split unevenly, with Quinn taking the larger share.

"Ha!" she barked, then dipped the piece in the plastic ramekin of honey and popped it in her mouth.

"Nicely done, Detective," he said, then dipped his much smaller piece and ate it.

"So why didn't you join the force down here once you moved? I imagine one of them would have been thrilled to have someone with your experience."

The air around them chilled so quickly one would have thought God himself had turned down the thermostat on the beach. Ian pulled his arms in and tapped a finger on the table's edge. He looked up at her, his expression contemplative, biting his bottom lip. "Would it be awful if I said that I didn't want to talk about it? I know you poured out your life story to me last night and that it seems a little unfair, but I'm just not ready."

A tight band contracted around Quinn's chest. She had clumsily stumbled into territory he was sensitive about. That much was obvious from the sober gaze he now held her with, instead of the bright one from just minutes before.

But why would a question about a job make someone that uncomfortable?

She knew her own reasons for feeling that way about her past, and none of them were good. Which meant Ian's probably weren't either. But in seconds she resolved that it didn't matter. She of all people would not force someone to share details about themselves they didn't want to revisit. She held up her hands in surrender. "You don't need to apologize. If anyone understands not wanting to talk about the past, it's me. You don't owe me anything. It's fine. I didn't mean to pry."

"No," he said, reaching out to cover her hand with his, sending an electric tingle up her arm, "you're not prying. There's nothing wrong with your question. And I know it's odd, me refusing to answer like that, but honesty's important to me. I could have just told you I was burned out, or wanted to try something different—"

"But those aren't the reasons why."

"They're part of it, but it would only be half the truth. And I don't want to start out like that with you."

Start out with me? Start what?

The prospect of the most likely answer to that question unnerved and energized her. Prompted by an overwhelming urge to deflect, she narrowed her eyes at him, adopting a sly expression. "You'd rather make it really weird and tell me straight up that you're hiding something?" she asked, her lips curving into a half-smile.

"Exactly," he said, the sparkle in his eyes from earlier returning as he lifted his hand from hers and started clearing the table.

≈

CLEARING up basically consisted of throwing all the take-out containers in the trash and putting the few dishes and glasses they had used into the dishwasher. Quinn slipped a soap pod into the machine and turned it on, swiveling to find Ian leaning against the counter, watching her.

"Thanks for dinner," he said.

"Um, I think that was you."

"Oh, yeah. Right." He smiled. "You're getting it next time."

"Definitely. I promise."

He pointed at her Riki unit sitting on the counter. "I've got one too. There's some pretty cool things you can do with it."

"Yeah?"

"I mean, who doesn't want a robot telling them a joke every morning?"

"Um, me?" Quinn replied, her eyebrows raised. "That sounds creepy."

"There's other fun stuff. I'll show you next time." He drummed the fingers of one hand on the granite countertop. "So what now? What's your next move in this thing?"

"Well, I can't just let it go."

"No. Especially given what Shane found in your trash.

Someone is definitely messing with you. You need to know why."

"What I *need* is to find out who was lying on my kitchen floor. I'm sure that's the key to all of this."

"Well, if you're open to it, I have an idea."

She nodded encouragingly. "What do you have in mind?"

"I don't think you're going to get any real help from the sheriff's department. Not after the display I saw this afternoon," Ian said.

"No, I suspect at this point they're more likely to arrest me than help me. I was considering going to see the District Attorney, but he's tied in so closely with the sheriff's department, I doubt I'll get very far with him."

"What if you went outside the county?"

"Where exactly were you thinking?"

"The Florida Department of Law Enforcement's headquarters are in Tallahassee. My brother—he's an attorney too—is pretty good friends with a special agent there. I can ask him to get in touch with her, see if she might be willing to help. Or at least give you some advice."

A little bubble of hope expanded within Quinn. "Yeah, that sounds great." But as soon as the words left her, reticence tugged at her heart. "Well...I don't know, Ian. Talking all this through with you is one thing, but you making calls for me—I don't know if it's fair for me to get you involved."

"I want to help. It's just a phone call. Maybe she can clear the path for you—or hey, get you a look at a missing persons list. Maybe somebody matches up with your description of the body."

"Well, I definitely got a good look. I won't forget him anytime soon."

"You think you'd recognize him if you saw a photo?"

The image of the man surfaced in her mind, the same way it did in her dreams. Light-brown, wide-set eyes. Blonde-brown hair, cut close, no sideburns. A short, pudgy nose and thick brows that nearly touched. 'Yeah, I'd definitely recognize him," she said.

He looked pleased. "Then think about it. If you decide you want me to call Jason—my brother—I will."

She leaned against the counter the same way he was and cocked her head. "So, your brother's a lawyer. You didn't mention that before."

"Well," he said, casually running a hand through his wavy hair. "I'm full of secrets."

"Mmmm. Clearly."

Quiet seconds followed as they held each other's gaze. Each beat of Quinn's heart seemed to pound louder in her ears until, mortified at the thought, she wondered if he might actually be able to hear it—

"So, um, I've got to be up pretty early for the morning crowd," he said, awkwardly pounding a fist lightly on the counter, then sidestepping toward the foyer, "so I should probably be going. But," he pointed at her as he went, "I'm going to hold you to that dinner you promised."

"I'll buy groceries and everything," she replied, following him. He spun to face her, pedaling backward toward the door until he grasped its handle. "Lock up after me. Turn on the alarm, okay?"

She nodded, then throwing caution aside blurted, "What are you doing tomorrow afternoon?"

His nose crinkled curiously. "Uh, working at The Shed. Like every Monday."

"Could you take a couple of hours off? Around three?"

"Why?"

"There's something I'd like to show you."

"You're not going to tell me?"

She fixed her face in a smirk, closing her eyelids halfway. "Guess I'm full of secrets too."

"Yes. Yes, you are," he said, his expression ripe with appreciation. He turned the handle and swung the door open, revealing an ever-darkening sky ushering in the approaching night. "Swing by and pick me up."

"I'll be there."

"Good night, Miss Bello," he said.

"Good night," she echoed as he pulled the door closed behind him, leaving her to lean against it, asking herself what in the world she was doing.

20

Because of the nature of the rental property business, Sundays and Mondays were the days that Quinn and Terri usually took off. On Sundays they used a message service to keep the phones running and receive alerts about any pressing issues tenants might have. But since most people considered Monday a workday, on that day Bello Realty employed a part-time receptionist in the office. They tended to cycle through a fair number of individuals provided by the temp agency. Presently, Kristin, a young woman in her early 20s, had held the job for the last eight weeks. She had done well, and Terri and Quinn both hoped she would stick around for a while, as retraining was always a headache.

On this Monday, Quinn decided to forego her normal routine and use the morning to catch up on some lingering paperwork and emails. With everything that happened on Saturday, starting with her visit to the sheriff's department, and then seeing Lena at the Hope Community Center, she had fallen a little behind. All the craziness was unsettling enough. She didn't want to lose her grip on the office too. Her plan was to spend a few hours there, get caught up and maybe even a little ahead of the game, so by the time she met Ian, she would feel productive and more in control. Who didn't feel better with a clear desk and inbox?

But at nine o'clock, all such hopes went out the window when she pulled into the parking lot of the Seaglass Cove Business Complex and saw a Wilson County Sheriff's Department patrol car parked directly in front of Unit #1D—home to Bello Realty.

"WHAT'S GOING ON?" Quinn asked as she barreled into the small lobby of Bello Realty. The room held a curved receptionist desk and four chairs around a black marble coffee table that displayed magazines, including the *Big Bend Travel Guide,* as well as a local real estate periodical listing properties for sale.

Kristin sat behind the reception desk, her eyes wide as a short man dressed in a beige suit turned away from her to face Quinn.

"Thank goodness you're here!" Kristin gushed, her breath heavy. "I was just about to call you."

"Is everything all right?" Quinn asked, her gaze targeted on the man. He had a ruddy complexion, pinched eyes and a severe crew cut. He held a black leather portfolio at his side.

"You're Quinn Bello?" he asked, his voice clipped.

"Yes, that's me. What's happened?" Her brain spun with a dozen awful scenarios.

Have Mom and Dad been hurt on their trip? Did something worse happen to Annalise's car, or—oh, no—to Annalise? Or Ian—no, they wouldn't contact me about that—

He flipped his wallet open, displaying a badge, then slipped it back inside his jacket. "I'm Investigator Mason Fisk of the Wilson County Sheriff's Department. I'm here about a fire that happened last night. Bello Realty owns 423 Piney Grove Lane, correct?"

Quinn's heart plummeted. Yes, they owned it. It had been a source of a lot of trouble in recent weeks.

"Yes, that's ours. You're telling me there's been a fire there?"

Thank goodness it's vacant right now. Maybe being unable to rent it was a blessing in disguise.

"No, not there," Investigator Fisk answered, shifting his weight. "Next door, at 421 Piney Grove."

Now Quinn's heart really tumbled. 421 Piney Grove was the *reason* she hadn't been able to lease 423 to anyone in the two months she had been there. The street was just a block from the beach and 423 was a lovely four-bedroom with a pool in the back and a view of the Gulf from the third floor. But the permanent residents of 421, the Kempers, who bought the place just six months earlier, had allowed the condition of their property to nose-dive, letting it wallow in a state of neglect. The grass was several inches high, the hedges untrimmed and wild, and mildew had begun spreading on the siding. Add to that three enormous dogs who attacked the chain-link fence viciously anytime anyone at 423 was in that backyard, and it had become impossible for Bello Realty to rent the 423 house. Her parents' repeated requests—and now hers—to the Kempers to correct the problems had gone unheeded, and while she had more than once desperately hoped, even prayed, that they would move, she wouldn't wish a fire on anyone.

"Are they all right? Was anyone hurt?" She remembered that the Kempers were in their late forties with no children at home, thank goodness.

"No. The alarm woke them. But the place is charred to a crisp. It'll have to be demolished, I'm sure."

"That's awful," Quinn replied, and she meant it. Friction aside, she was wondering whether she should offer the Kempers the use of the 423 property until they could make other arrangements, when Investigator Fisk interrupted her train of thought.

"You've been having a dispute with the Kempers, is that correct?"

"A dispute? Well, I don't know if I'd call it a dispute. Ever since they moved in they've just let their property fall apart. And with those unruly dogs, it's been nearly impossible to rent our property. No one wants to take a vacation and look at or hear that. We've been asking them to clean it up for a while now, mow, maybe bring the dogs in sometimes—"

"The Kempers say you've been sending aggressive emails. Threatening them."

"What?" Her center hardened. She didn't like where this was going. It was the last two days on repeat.

Am I about to be blamed for something else?

"That's ridiculous," she said bitingly, her voice rising a half-step. "I haven't sent any threatening emails. My parents handled the issue before I took over, and since then I've sent reasonable, justified requests, asking the Kempers to make a few corrections to put the property back into the condition it was in before they bought it. I haven't sent them anything remotely like a threat."

"The Kempers have identified you as the only person they could think of with a grudge against them."

"A grudge...wait, are you telling me this fire was arson?"

"We believe so, ma'am. And according to the Kempers, you've not only got a motive to do it, but you essentially threatened as much in your last emails."

Adrenaline and confusion raced through Quinn as she absorbed what he was insinuating. "You think *I* burned down their house? With them in it?" Her heart skipped a beat. Then another. She tried to ignore it.

"Are you maintaining that you didn't send a threatening email?"

"Yes, that's exactly what I'm maintaining!" Out of the corner of her eye, she caught a glimpse of Kristin, looking even more like a deer in the headlights than before. It occurred to her that she couldn't see Kristin's hands, prompting Quinn to wonder whether the twenty-something was recording the whole thing on her cell phone, somewhere out of sight below the desk. She wasn't sure if that was a good or bad thing, and registered that she needed to keep her cool, just in case.

"Do you mind showing me your email account right now? We might be able to clear this up, shine a light on what's going on."

Quinn's mind began whirling at breakneck speed, evaluating the situation. She didn't have to show him anything. He didn't have a warrant. Her computer and email account were private. He was asking, but she didn't have to agree to his request.

Or she could just say yes, especially since she knew there was nothing in her account that would remotely qualify as a threat against the Kempers. But as an attorney she also knew it was almost always better to make law enforcement jump through the proper hoops to avoid any sort of confusion or unwarranted invasion of privacy.

The Kempers must have been able to produce the threatening emails for him. Otherwise he wouldn't be here now, trying to verify that they existed on Quinn's account as well, eliminating the possibility that someone else sent them. Of course, he would eventually serve a warrant on the email provider seeking those records, but finding them this morning on Quinn's computer was a much quicker way to do that. The problem was that once she showed him there weren't any such emails on her computer, that wouldn't be the end of it. He would likely still collect the computer as evidence to have it searched for deleted data.

The reality was that she could say no and insist on a

warrant, but that would just drag things out. And there was always the possibility that if she said no, he would force the issue anyway by declaring that "exigent circumstances" existed, meaning that unless he acted immediately she would have the means and opportunity to delete any evidence of incriminating emails. In this case, expediency and appearing to be cooperative seemed the best route. Possibly having her computer confiscated wouldn't be convenient, but maybe she could learn something from him in the course of their interaction that would help her convince him to not handle it that way.

Praying she wasn't making a mistake, she pressed her shoulders back. "I'm assuming the alleged emails are supposed to have come from my work email account?"

He glanced at his phone. "qbello@bellorealty.com."

"Yeah, that's my work email. I can show you that. But I don't know what good it will do. If I had sent the emails, which I didn't, I could have just deleted them. You should just request the records from my email provider."

"True. But I'll check the deleted files on the computer while I'm here and go from there. Unless, you'd rather I get a warrant. But I'll have to stay here while we wait for it and detain you. Just to protect the evidence."

Quinn sighed exasperatedly. "No. Let's just get this over with," she said as she stepped past him, heading for the short hallway leading to her office.

INVESTIGATOR FISK SAT in the soft, white leather chair behind Quinn's glass-topped desk, while she stood behind him, eyeing the screen of her desktop PC over his shoulder. He had asked if he could be the one to actually operate the computer, which Quinn knew was to prevent her from tampering with anything.

It only took seconds for Fisk to navigate to the mail application and open it. He enlarged the resulting window which listed an inbox, sent box, outbox, spam and trash box for the account "qbello@bellorealty.com." He typed "jkrkkemper@earthmail.com" in the search box, which Quinn recognized as the Kempers' email address, then punched the "Enter" key.

The window refreshed, pulling up a list of all emails to and from Quinn and the Kempers. As Quinn expected there were about a dozen of them, with the earliest dated two months ago, right around when she took over the company. What she hadn't expected were the two emails listed as the most recent ones: one sent by her to the Kempers two days ago—on Saturday—and one sent yesterday.

A sweat broke over Quinn. She hadn't sent any emails to the Kempers on Saturday or Sunday. In fact, the last email she had sent to them had gone out more than a week earlier. Without a word to Quinn, Investigator Fisk clicked, opening both of the suspect emails.

The first from Saturday read:

Mr. and Mrs. Kemper,
Despite our attempts to get you to rectify conditions at your residence, you have completely ignored us. I can't allow the property at 423 to sit unrented in perpetuity because you refuse to clean up your squalor and control those unruly dogs. You are forcing my hand. You should take me seriously. If you know who I am and what I am capable of, then you know I am not bluffing. If you do not reply immediately with plans to correct the situation I will have no choice but to take serious action. You are undermining me and my success in this company. I will not stand for it or allow you to ruin my business. I will not allow this to go on. This is your last warning.

Sincerely,
Quinn Bello

The next one, sent on Sunday, read:

Mr. and Mrs. Kemper,
As it has been over 24 hours and I have received no reply from you,
I take it that you are refusing to act to correct the issues on your
property which are so drastically affecting the value and appeal of
our property at 423. You have left me no option. You have no one to
blame but yourselves. I am tired of being pushed around and
ignored. Don't say I didn't warn you.

Sunday's email was unsigned.

Quinn shivered as the import of these emails sank in. She
should have known better. She should have insisted on a
warrant. And a lawyer. She should not have tried to advise
herself. The old adage was definitely true: *He who represents
himself has a fool for a client.*

And what a fool she'd been.

21

Quinn held her head in her hands, elbows propped on the metal table in the same interview room at the Sheriff's Department she had been in with Shane less than twenty-four hours earlier. Only now, Investigator Fisk sat across from her, with a stack of paper and binder before him as he stared her down. She dug the tips of her fingers into her forehead, willing away the murderous headache that had overtaken her half an hour ago. It didn't help. Giving up, she ran the hand over her thick hair, today hanging loose to her shoulders. She expelled a huff and blinked before determinedly meeting Fisk's stare.

"I don't know any other way to say it," she said. "I didn't write those emails. Someone else did. Someone broke into the office, or somehow hacked my account and sent them as if they were me."

"Why would anybody do that?"

"*That* is a great question, Investigator. One of many I've been asking for days now! Why would there be a dead body on my floor? Why would somebody be following me around town? Why would they vandalize my neighbor's car and pin it on me by stashing the evidence in my trash? Don't you see a pattern here?"

"I do, but not the pattern you want me to see."

Quinn bit back a growl. *Same song, second verse.* "You've been talking to Shane Cody."

"Deputy Cody has filled me in on things, but he's not the only one connecting the dots the same way." Fisk tapped the stack of papers. "These emails show a deliberate intention to do something harmful to the Kempers. Arson would fit the bill. It would definitely remove the Kempers from the 421 property."

Quinn couldn't stifle the laugh that escaped her throat. "Are you being serious right now? Do you think it will be any easier to rent out our property now that it's beside a burned-out shell or the eventual construction site that'll replace it? Arson solves nothing for me."

"But if the Kempers move away and don't come back, the dogs will be gone and there'll be a bright, shiny house next door. Maybe that's what you were counting on."

"If that was my plan do you think I'd leave those emails on my computer? Why wouldn't I erase them?"

He leaned forward, the table edge pressing into his midsection. "Maybe you're not thinking straight." He eyed her with the same accusatory gleam that had shone from Shane's eyes the night before. "You do have a history of acting irrationally, exhibiting paranoia, putting others at risk, drinking—"

"Good grief! What do I have to do to convince you people that *I'm not on anything!*"

"There's no need to start yelling, Ms. Bello. You're going to want to calm down."

She sniffed a loud breath in through her nose, held it briefly, then blew it out through a tiny circle she made with her lips. Taking stock of her posture, she also dropped her shoulders from where they were jammed up by her ears. *He's right. I've got to keep my cool if there's any hope of convincing them I'm not some tightly-wound maniac that goes off and does something crazy whenever I get angry.*

"I'm not impaired, Investigator," she said, keeping her voice low and steady. "I am thinking completely clearly. What you're referring to—the incident in Tampa—that happened after a long period of mixing prescriptions and self-medicating. I'm better now."

"What about the vodka we found in your trash?"

Quinn breathed in through gritted teeth. "It. Isn't. Mine." The mention of the vodka bottle brought another question to mind. "Did you find my prints on the paint can?" Her prints were conveniently in the system, both from when she was admitted to the Florida Bar and when she was arrested in Tampa. It wouldn't have taken them long to make the match.

"As a matter of fact, no."

"See! I told you—"

"Actually there were no prints on the can at all." He eyed her accusingly. "Wiped clean."

Quinn took his meaning, and raised her eyebrows. "And you think, what, that I wiped my prints off, then threw it in my trash?"

"That's one explanation."

"Because that's what they want you to think!"

"Who's *they*?" Fisk asked.

"I don't know. Whoever is following me. Whoever is setting me up."

"Again, why would anyone do that?" he pressed.

"Your guess is as good as mine. And I really wish you guys would start trying to guess at another explanation besides it all being *me*. Maybe I know something I shouldn't, or have something I shouldn't, or—here's a crazy idea—found a dead body that disappeared and won't let the issue go. Somebody wants me to stop asking questions and all this is designed to make that happen, or make me seem unreliable, or worse, guilty, if I won't. All this started with that body and—"

The door opened and a young deputy entered, handed Fisk a sheet of paper, and walked out without saying a word.

"What is that?" Quinn asked, nodding at the sheet.

Fisk ignored her question, finished reading the paper, then looked up. "We obtained a warrant for your vehicle and home, Ms. Bello. We found an empty gasoline can and several containers of lighter fluid—all but one used up—in the padlocked storage chest of your pickup truck."

"Those are not mine."

"Right. Just like everything else? No, I'm sure someone got a key to the padlock and put them in there," he said, his tone thick with sarcasm.

Quinn leaned back from the table, crossing her arms. "We're done here. Am I under arrest or am I free to go?"

"Actually, you are being charged. One count of malicious destruction of property arising out of the damage done to the Sardises' Mercedes."

Disbelief surged through Quinn. "Based on what you found in the trash? Which was accessible by anyone?"

"Not just that, no." Fisk slid an iPad out from his binder and cued up a video, then spun it so Quinn could see.

The video was black-and-white CCTV footage. The view was from on high, giving a wide shot of a parking lot and, farther in the background across Highway 98, almost half of Bello Breakers. It showed the back side of Number Five, Number Four—Quinn's house—and half of Number Three. The scene was dark, the night lit by the parking lot lights and the street lamps along Bello Breakers Circle. Quinn had a pretty good idea where the footage had come from.

"That's the parking lot of The Cove Hotel, across the street from my house," she said, leaning closer to the iPad and squinting. She looked up at Fisk from beneath her lashes. "Where did you get this?"

"The hotel was happy to cooperate. Thought we'd give it a shot and," he tapped the screen and the video began to play, "we got lucky."

The time stamp read just after one a.m. on Sunday morning. A single vehicle drove past on the beach highway, its headlights cutting through the dark before moving off-screen. Fisk had obviously queued the video to the relevant point, because only seconds passed before, in the distant background, someone emerged from the side yard between Quinn's house and Number Five, the house rented by the Sardises. The person appeared to be female, dressed in dark clothes and wearing gloves, with her hair pulled back into a thick ponytail—just the way Quinn's looked when she wore hers in one. A sickening punch pummeled Quinn. Had she not known better—had she not known she had been in bed at one in the morning and not prowling around outside—she would have thought the person on the screen was her.

"That's not me," Quinn protested.

Fisk said nothing.

The figure held something in her hand as she walked over to the Sardises' driveway and around to the driver's side of the Mercedes. Though most of the figure's body was blocked by the car, her movements were clearly that of someone defacing the vehicle with spray paint. After about thirty seconds, she walked over to Quinn's trash receptacle, tossed the spray can in, then returned the way she came, disappearing into the darkness between the two houses.

"I see you chose to go back into the house from the beach, not the rear entrance. Smart. That way if someone caught sight of you coming and going from the Sardises' place, you could argue the figure could be anyone coming from the beach. Did you know the hotel has CCTV cameras?"

"That *was* someone coming from the beach. That was not me!"

He ignored her denial. "Are the cans from your truck clean too, or are we going to find your prints this time? If you talk to me, Quinn, I can help you."

A cyclone of panic, anger, and confusion swirled within her as she clamped her mouth shut, staring him down.

"Fine," Fisk muttered and rose, his chair grinding against the tile floor with an ear-piercing screech. He read Quinn her rights in a brisk monotone before detailing the charges against her. "Because the damage to the vehicle exceeds five hundred dollars, the destruction of property offense is a felony. You're also being charged with misdemeanor trespass. You'll be processed and allowed to post bail, then, if you want to try to do this the easy way, we can talk and maybe keep the damage you've done to yourself to a minimum."

"And the arson charge? I assume that's coming?" she asked.

"Getting our ducks in a row," Fisk answered drolly.

Quinn's head throbbed, the explosive pressure from earlier continuing to mount. Her hand moved to her temple, rubbing it as she tried to force clarity. She knew she had to get control, think logically, and work the situation if she was going to have any chance of clearing this up. She took a calming breath, reminding herself who she was and what she was trained to do. Then she folded her arms, sat up straight and pierced Fisk with her gaze.

"I'm done talking. I want an attorney. And I want my phone call."

THE BOOKING PROCESS was completely humiliating. Not only because it meant she once again found herself on the wrong side of the law, but because it was in Seaglass Cove. Her hometown. The place where she had sought refuge. All the bad things the people in that place had believed about her for years were now being proved true. Again.

Only they aren't true this time.

She wondered if Ian would stand by her after the mountain of evidence they were uncovering against her. *Probably not*, she thought wistfully. He'd have to be as crazy as they thought she was to do that.

This arrest also rekindled all the trauma of her experience in Tampa. Frisked, again. Booking photo, again. Fingerprinted, again. Holding cell, again. Phone call to an attorney, again.

This time Quinn didn't have a law firm at her disposal, so instead she placed a call to a local attorney, one her family had used on multiple real estate transactions. He didn't do criminal work, but would be able to help her out initially, then connect her with the right person. For now she just wanted someone on her side, advising her through this nightmare. Unfortunately, he wasn't available, and she left an urgent message with his secretary explaining the situation and asking him to come to the jail as soon as possible.

They put her back in the holding cell after she made her call, and Quinn expected they might leave her there for a while to let her stew. But to her surprise, they retrieved her after only fifteen minutes to allow her to post bond. The jail bond schedule set the combined bail at $2,500, which she was able to pay with her credit card, securing her freedom at least for now.

"You sure you don't want to sit down and talk about this? You confess to the arson and the rest of it, and things will go easier for you," Fisk said, leaning nonchalantly on the counter while Quinn's belongings were returned to her—her purse, phone and pepper spray, all logged and inventoried when she had been searched.

Scribbling her name on the electronic pad to acknowledge receipt of her belongings, she tossed them in her bag and slung it over her shoulder. Then she turned on Fisk, her face set hard in the same dogged expression she adopted when grilling adversarial witnesses on the stand. "You're not attempting to question me after I've invoked my right to counsel, are you Investigator? Because that would be a clear violation of my Miranda rights and taint any information you might obtain, violating what I assume passes for procedure around here."

"You're no longer in custody, so that doesn't apply as you well know. And I'm just offering you a chance to make things right. Get it off your chest," he countered. There was something so smug, so satisfied about his expression, it made her want to slap it off him.

"Mmm-hmm," she mumbled. "Well, what I know is that I'm still in the building concluding my custodial hold, and that you just initiated questioning again with a detained person who has invoked her right to counsel. I suggest you stop before I file a complaint with the department for harassment and procedural violations intended to manipulate a confession. I'm leaving, unless I'm now under arrest for arson too?"

Fisk folded his arms in front of him. "Not yet," he said, but his eyes might as well have added, *but that's coming.*

She wrapped him in an icy stare. "You're going about this the wrong way. The people responsible are going to slip away because you can't see farther than the nose on your face. If you'd even consider that maybe I'm being set up, you could actually do some good here. Instead, you're making an innocent person's life a nightmare."

Without giving Fisk an opportunity to respond, Quinn strode past him to the exit, so close that their shoulders nearly brushed. She refused to swerve so much as a millimeter, determined that not even her gait was going to suggest she was the slightest bit intimidated or unnerved.

After all, if she was going to live life labeled, branded, and categorized a liar, she might as well earn it.

22

_____

Quinn walked out of the sheriff's department into the blinding light of the midday sun to see Ian Wolfe leaning against her truck in the parking lot. He sported dark-washed jeans, a loose, white button-down with sleeves rolled up to his elbows and work boots. Combined with the aviator sunglasses and that perfect wavy hair, he looked like he had been ripped straight off a movie screen.

"*What* are you doing here?" she asked as she neared him, her heart welling with relief at the sight of him.

"I hear the sheriff's department is a great place to pick up women in this town," he answered, removing his sunglasses and stepping away from the truck.

She raised her eyebrows. "Oh, really?"

"Yep. At least that's the word down at The Shed."

"Seriously, what are you doing here?"

"Seriously, someone came into The Shed talking about a fire, possible arson, and that you'd been brought in for questioning. I thought you might need a little support."

She didn't know whether to laugh or cry. "How in the world are people already talking about this? It literally *just* happened."

"I think your receptionist may have called a friend or two. Or ten," he said.

"Oh, wow." *So much for keeping Kristin on.*

"And I'm pretty sure she posted a video online."

Quinn's mouth dropped. "You're kidding."

Ian's lips rolled inward as if biting back a retort. He held his phone out and pressed an icon. The footage of Quinn being questioned by Fisk when she first arrived at the office played.

Quinn's insides melted. "Good grief," she muttered, shaking her head.

"So what happened in there?" he asked, inclining his head toward the building.

"Short version? They charged me with a felony for the vandalism of the Sardises' Mercedes and, if they have their way, they'll be charging me with arson next."

Incredulity creased every inch of Ian's face. "Say what, now?"

"You heard me," she replied.

"I think I'd better hear the long version."

IAN TOOK her to The Shed, where he set Quinn down at a table in the back office and listened while she rehashed the insane events of the morning. He had the cook prepare two thick roast beef sandwiches on sourdough with hefty tomato slices and fresh lettuce, but the food sat nearly untouched before them. Quinn downed her latte, however, within two minutes of getting it. Now she sipped water through a straw, grinding the top between her teeth as Ian spoke.

"This has gone way too far," he said, bending his head toward her, as if emphasizing his point. "You really need to secure representation right away to protect yourself."

"I've reached out to the attorney our family has always used," she said. "Criminal law's not his thing, but he'll be able to recommend someone."

"Whoever this is—the person setting you up—they aren't messing around. Arson? Someone could've been killed." Concern clouded his dark-grey eyes.

"I don't think they're too worried about killing someone. Going by the corpse on my floor, anyway."

As if by reflex, his hand moved in the direction of hers, but at the last second diverted to wrap around his glass of tea instead. He sniffed and shifted in his seat. "I don't want you to be next. If the authorities are bent on blaming you and refuse to figure out why you're being targeted, then you've got to get someone on your side that will."

"The attorney," she said.

"I was thinking more like a private detective."

Quinn sighed. "I don't know if I can afford that."

"What about your parents? I'm sure—"

"No. Absolutely not. I am not doing this to them again. They had to help out last time when I ran out of cash. Thank goodness they're off on a European river cruise right now and out of touch. I've sworn Terri to secrecy—threatened her with losing her job if she so much as texts them about any of this, but I don't know if that'll stop her. She knows I'm bluffing."

"What about the Seaglass Cove rumor mill?" he asked. "Won't it reach them?"

"I'll have to hope Mom and Dad aren't checking messages regularly. I mean, I know word will get to them eventually. Just hopefully later rather than sooner." She looked at the time on her phone. It was almost one o'clock. "Look, I know I asked you to go with me at three, but I need to do something to take my mind off of things until I hear back from the lawyer or I'm going to go stir-crazy. Do you think you could leave with me now?"

"Hmm," he said, eyeing her wryly. "I'll have to ask the boss. But I think I can swing it."

23

Ian sat in the passenger seat of Quinn's truck, keeping his head forward but cutting his gaze sideways at her while she drove. Her thick red hair was down today, flowing in waves that fell just below her shoulders, the sun glinting off flyaway ends, turning them golden. Her lips—with their bubble-gum color and deep cupid's bow—fluttered as she ranted about Investigator Fisk and Shane and the arson charges looming as she drove them to their mystery destination. It was incredibly distracting and he worked to stay focused on what she was saying.

Cool air blew through the vents as she talked animatedly, one hand on the wheel while gesturing with the other. She alternated between them, her shapely fingers dancing in space, a gloss with just a hint of palest peach on her nails. She was spirited, that was for sure. Even despite the brokenness he sensed in her and the fear she had to be fighting, she was holding it together. She was scrappy and he admired that. Was drawn to it even.

But she had allowed herself to be vulnerable too, sharing all the ugly details of her past that night at The Shed. He thought he understood why. Theirs was a new friendship and he was one of the few people who seemed to trust her. She wanted them to start off on the sure footing of the truth.

Guilt, like a cold cube of ice, slipped into his stomach. He, on the other hand, had not been as forthcoming that evening. Or the evening after. While she seemingly spared nothing, he continued holding his cards close to his chest. It didn't seem quite fair, and not for the first time, he felt like he was cheating by not telling her. But the fact was, he simply couldn't bring himself to do it.

When she made a hard right turn, pulling into the parking lot of Hope Community Church as he was thinking about cheating, he almost laughed out loud at the irony.

He also couldn't help but wonder if maybe this was God's way of telling him it was time to spill it.

24

Quinn maneuvered through the church parking lot, slowing at one point to allow a pedestrian to pass.

"Church?" Ian asked, his eyes scrunching as he turned to look at her.

"Is that a problem?" She was careful to keep her tone curious, not judgmental.

He pursed his lips and shook his head. "Not in the slightest. My faith's the only thing that got me through—" He cut himself off, his neck turning pink before he recovered. "Well, through life."

Quinn's intrigue meter pinged. Ian was definitely holding something back. Once more she wondered what his backstory was. Given his guardedness, it might hold a tale as interesting as hers. If interesting was the right word for it.

"I know the feeling," she replied, glossing over his clear omission.

"I actually miss going," he said. "I just haven't gotten around to finding a place that fits since I moved down here."

"Well, you ought to give this place a try," Quinn said, gesturing at the church building. "I've been coming here practically my whole life. Buuuut," she said, drawing the word out, "that's not where we're headed today." She continued past the church to the parking lot in front of the adjacent building.

"Hope Community Center," Ian read off the sign posted over its doors. "People say good things about this place."

"They should. They do amazing work here." She turned off the engine and swiveled toward him. "Next to kayaking, coming here is the thing that gives me the most perspective. And I could use some of that right now."

"Who couldn't?" he quipped.

"Well, then come on," she said, releasing her seat belt and letting it snap back into place. "There are some people I want you to meet."

FOR REASONS she couldn't fathom, nerves fluttered in Quinn's stomach as she stood in the gym of the Hope Community Center making introductions. "Ian, this is Lena Sharp, the Hope Community Center Director, and her son, Jamie, and daughter, Keisha." She swallowed hard, hoping the nervousness wasn't visible on her face.

Keisha, only seven and a bit shy, stood behind Lena, while Jamie, ten years old and quite protective of his mother, thrust his hand out for Ian to shake. Quinn caught the hint of a smile threatening to break out on Ian's face, but saw that he dampened it, instead adopting a serious expression to match Jamie's. He obviously wanted the boy to feel he was being taken seriously. It was incredibly endearing.

"Nice to meet you, Jamie. Keisha." Ian's eyes flicked to Lena. "And you, Lena. Quinn tells me you're the best friend she has in Seaglass Cove."

Lena's finely groomed eyebrows rose, wrinkling her forehead. "Did she now?"

"Can we go start the cans, Mom?" asked Keisha, tugging on her mother's shirt.

"Sure, baby, go on," Lena answered.

Calling out a quick, "Bye, Quinn," as they went, the children ran to the opposite side of the gym where a dozen tables were positioned in an assembly line. Each one was covered with different foodstuffs—canned food, produce and dry goods. A few adults were bringing more boxes of supplies from the kitchen, either in their arms or on dollies, continuing to add more items to the tables. Jamie and Keisha had moved to a table crowded with assorted canned vegetables and were stacking them by type.

"So explain to me what we've got going here," Ian said.

Lena pointed to a mountain of empty cardboard boxes on the floor beside the first table. "Every week the Hope Center puts together boxes made up of food donations and additional groceries we've purchased with monetary donations. Each box holds enough food for a family of five for an entire week."

"That's amazing," Ian said, his eyes roving over the assembly line. "I didn't realize there was that much need in this town."

"We don't only serve Seaglass Cove. People from all over the county with all different kinds of stories come here when they find themselves at a place in life where they need a little help. Some are long-term clients, some just need to get over a hump. Some have lost jobs, some haven't held a job in years. We've got families who have spent every last dime on cancer treatment and veterans who are still struggling years after discharge."

"How do you work it out? Who gets a box, I mean?"

"We don't. If someone walks in and says they need one, they get a box. That's all there is to it," Lena said, satisfaction shining in her eyes.

Quinn loved to hear Lena gush about this ministry and watch her passion for it overflow onto yet another person. The way it had overflowed onto her. "Everybody, every time," Quinn said, smiling at Lena.

"Everybody, every time," Lena echoed, grinning back.

"You know," Ian piped in, "every week we have extra food at The Shed—produce, baked goods, other stuff—that we aren't going to use for one reason or another. If you accept donations from restaurants—"

"Oh, we do," Quinn and Lena answered simultaneously, prompting them both to laugh.

"Then I'd like to help," Ian said.

"Fantastic," Lena replied. "Just drop off whatever you have by Monday morning. As you can see, we start setting up around noon and then get the assembly line moving around two. Our clients begin turning up around four o'clock to collect their boxes."

"Well, starting next week, you can count on The Little Red Shed to help out with those supplies. But for now," he said, rubbing his hands together, "I'm all yours. Put me to work."

25

Ian was surprised at how fast the work was done, and that by three thirty, the boxes were nearly all packed up and ready to be handed out. Quinn was still helping Keisha and Jamie with the last few, making sure they had the same amount of provisions that the first boxes did. She explained that sometimes there had to be substitutions because they would run out of one thing or another. Ian finished moving the completed boxes closer to the door where the Center's clients would soon be arriving to claim them. He loved that the program chose to use the term 'client' to refer to those they were assisting. Charitable aid and preservation of dignity should always go hand in hand.

After stacking the last of the completed boxes in rows, he paused to lean against the wall, taking a swig from a water bottle Lena had given him. He had actually worked up quite a sweat and ran the back of his hand across his forehead to wipe away the beads gathered there. He hadn't planned on manual labor today, and although his work boots were well-suited to it, the shirt he wore wasn't. Smears of dirt and dust from carrying and shifting boxes streaked his white button-down, and he was pretty sure that by now he had sweat right through it. He cringed a little. Not exactly the look he was going for. Then again, Quinn was so busy with the kids, she probably hadn't even noticed.

He felt the corners of his mouth rise as he watched her. She was chasing Keisha now, tickling her when she caught her and laughing, throwing her head back. A warm buzz filled his center. Even now, with all that was hanging over her head, *this* was how Quinn Bello chose to spend her time. Filling the void of uncertainty by caring for others. By bringing a little girl joy. By refusing to bow to the wave of trouble rushing toward her. That was the kind of woman worth getting to know. The kind of woman worth breaking his rule for.

His gaze stayed on Quinn and Keisha as the little girl grabbed Quinn's hand and led her to the last table which held pens, crayons, paper, and what looked like folded cards.

"That's our note table," Lena said as she came up behind him unannounced. "We write notes of encouragement, scripture, prayers for the client on the card. Sometimes the kids color pictures on them. Every client gets one."

"That's really lovely," Ian said, his gaze swiveling back to Quinn. She was bent over a card now, scribbling something in earnest.

Lena leaned against the wall beside Ian. "Quinn told me what's been going on," she said.

"She did?" Ian asked, not exactly sure which recent events Lena was referring to. And whether he was one of them.

"Yep. All the stuff with the sheriff's department. And the corpse on her floor—something she initially failed to tell me. And now the arson."

"It's insane," Ian remarked disdainfully.

"She said you're helping her."

Ian's eyes flicked to Lena. "I'm trying. I'm not really sure what I can do, though."

"Well, I don't either. But what I do know is that you are the first person besides me that Quinn has spent more than fifteen minutes with since she came back to Seaglass Cove."

Ian forced himself to not look too pleased. "Really?"

"Really. What do you think that means, Ian?"

He shrugged. "I have no idea."

"Me either. But, Ian, I am really, *really,* hoping that you will stick around to find out."

26

"I want to thank you for taking me to the Center today," Ian said, rotating in the passenger seat so he was facing Quinn as they sat together in her pickup in the parking lot of The Shed. "I hate that I wasn't aware of the program sooner."

"Thanks for going. Not everyone would be that excited about being dragged away from work to do more work," she said wryly, though she absolutely meant it. He truly seemed to enjoy being a part of what they accomplished that afternoon. And he really worked hard—as evidenced by his rumpled, sweat-stained shirt, and the smears of dirt across his forehead and forearms that he either hadn't noticed or hadn't bothered to wipe away. Even his hair was showing signs of exertion with its unruly, curly ends more pronounced than usual, likely unleashed by the umpteen number of times he must have run a hand through it while working.

And he had never looked better.

"Well, I was happy to do it," he said. "And I hope you'll ask me again. Or I might just show up uninvited."

"Well, I might just be okay with that," she said, the response leaping from her mouth before she could stop it. She felt heat flush her face and prayed it hadn't turned red.

If it had, Ian didn't react. "Will you let me know when your lawyer gets in touch, and what he says?"

She nodded.

"I'm not feeling great about you going home alone," he said, worry simmering in those grey eyes which she was becoming more and more in danger of being lost in. "Are you sure you don't want to come inside and hang out? It's trivia night, so even though we aren't serving a full dinner menu, I have to be here because we'll be swamped. Otherwise I'd go with you—"

"I'm fine," she assured him, and she really was. Strangely enough, she felt more empowered now than ever, certain after the latest events that she wasn't imagining things. "I'll lock up the house. And turn on the alarm. I'll be perfectly safe."

"Don't forget what we talked about. There's a reason this is happening. Go over everything you can think of and make a list until something jumps out at you. Your lawyer's going to want that anyway," he said.

"I will, I promise."

He reached out, covering her hand with his, sending a jolt of electricity through her. Though her heart was drumming, she kept her breathing in check as he leaned in slightly. "You'll figure it out. And I'll do whatever I can to help, Quinn. Okay?"

She nodded, pressing her lips together to avoid saying anything embarrassing as he slipped out of the truck. When he reached the back door to The Shed he glanced back one last time and waved before disappearing inside, triggering Quinn to exhale the breath she hadn't realized she was holding.

AN HOUR LATER, Quinn sat at her kitchen table with her cell phone, laptop and a legal pad. After first making a trip to the grocery store—she wasn't going to be unprepared the next time Ian came by—she set up shop, determined to stay put until she figured something out.

The family lawyer finally called around six, apologizing for the delay and recommending a well-known criminal lawyer in Tallahassee to represent her, given the small-town runaround she was facing. In his opinion an outsider wouldn't be swayed by the local sheriff's department and could exert more pressure on them to take her claims seriously. He had put in a call to the Tallahassee lawyer, but hadn't heard back yet. He promised to let her know as soon as he did, but to contact him in the meantime if the authorities arrested her again or called her in for questioning. So, at least for the moment, that issue had stalled.

This left her alone in the locked-up, alarmed-up house, planted at the table with a ginger ale and dinner of cheese, Honeycrisp apple slices, and nuts, trying to divine who would do this to her. At the top of the page she had listed a dozen or so clients and defendants who might have a grudge. The clients were those who were unhappy about the outcomes of their cases after losing while being represented by Quinn. The defendants were those Quinn won judgments against—two construction companies, a doctor, a couple of privately held businesses and a few individuals in deadly traffic cases whose property had been seized and sold to pay the judgments owed to her clients. Each of these cases involved amounts well over a million dollars, providing ample motive for a desire for payback.

But staring at the list, Quinn couldn't shake the sense that this just didn't feel right. What was happening to her was too complicated a scenario, too involved for someone who just wanted payback. There were easier ways to do that—key her car, trash her house, troll her social media accounts. What was going on in Seaglass Cove felt too sophisticated for mere revenge.

If not for revenge, then why?

The other standard motives for criminal acts were love, hate, money, and concealment. Love didn't make sense. Its antithesis, hate, didn't come into play either. Who hated her on a personal level? Not her ex. Simon had been the one to break things off, not her. He didn't hate her. Other than sending her those stupid flowers, he hadn't shown signs of caring at all.

But what about Shane Cody? He's made it pretty clear that he hates me.

The thought left her slightly ashamed. Yes, Shane still had hard feelings over what happened with Annie. But would that incite him to carry out a vendetta like this? He *was* perfectly positioned to do it, but still, it seemed a gigantic stretch. He was a law enforcement officer, after all, and a good one, as far as she knew.

Nevertheless, she jotted his name down. She wasn't in a position to rule anyone out at this point. With that in mind, she went ahead and wrote "Annie Cody's family members" after Shane's name, the guilt she had carried since that night eighteen years ago weighing heavy on her as she did.

Liar. Thief. Delinquent. User. Loser.

The labels scrolled through her head like a mantra. She pushed them aside and took a sip of ginger ale, willing herself to focus on the task at hand. Unable to come up with any other suspects possibly motivated by love, hate, or revenge, she was left with money and concealment.

What monetary gain could there be in someone framing me?

Who would benefit financially if she was crowned a crazy person, unreliable, a drunk or user, convicted and jailed for vandalism and arson.

No one.

She was only the manager of Bello Realty. She didn't own it or any of the properties. Her going to jail wouldn't result in any of the property being sold, so acquiring real estate couldn't be a driving force. She was broke, so there wasn't any money for someone to get their hands on if she suddenly was out of the picture.

Which left concealment, a motive that would mean all of these steps were being taken to keep something from coming to light. But what?

She tapped the side of her glass, a trickle of sweat dripping down to meet the table's surface. Looking up from her notes, she watched the distant surf through the windows at the back of the house, white foam crashing over and over, the thunder of it a faint roar behind the closed French doors.

If I assume concealment is the motive, then either I already know something incriminating or damaging to someone's interests and don't realize it, or someone is afraid I'll eventually discover something damaging if I'm allowed to continue on as I am.

But what could I know, or be on the verge of discovering?

How was she supposed to guess what she might know already, but not recognize as a threat to someone? She blew out a frustrated whoosh of breath. It was impossible.

Instead, she tried focusing on the theory that she was positioned to learn something or gain information that someone didn't want her to have. Which begged the question, how would setting her up protect the information from coming to light?

That was the first easy question she had come across. By discrediting her, by showing her to be a liar, a loose cannon, someone still unreliable and at odds with the law, they could make sure no one took her seriously. So, if and when she finally put two and two together and became aware of the damaging information she was privy to, it wouldn't matter, because no one would believe her if she tried to expose it.

Of course, the other option was that they were setting her up to create a narrative for eliminating her before she could do any harm. It wouldn't be a far reach to use everything that was happening to paint her as a depressed, out-of-control woman. Then they could kill her to keep her from talking, and make it look like a suicide. It was a story people would believe, given all she had gone through and was going through now. Tendrils of fear wove through her bones like vines climbing a trellis.

Is that what's happening? Am I being set up to die for knowing something I don't even realize I know? And how exactly did I discover, or am I going to discover, this information?

No one had approached her or reached out to her in any way that was out of the norm. There had been no letters, no stop-bys at work, no threats or notes slipped into the mailbox.

But there have been phone calls, a small voice inside reminded her. *Phone calls with no one on the other end of the line.*

"Those were telemarketers," she mumbled aloud. "Not espionage."

But were they? What if there was something to Ian's suggestion the other night at The Shed that the calls had been someone's attempts to get a hold of her? Attempts that failed because the caller initially got cold feet when she *did* answer, and then, once he finally found the courage to try again, she had stopped answering unrecognized numbers.

She put herself in their shoes. *If I absolutely had to share information with someone, but had to do it under the radar so it wouldn't be detected, how would I do it if the person wouldn't take my calls?*

The answer came to her immediately.

Quinn's fingers flew over her laptop keyboard as she pulled up her accounts on Facebook and Twitter, scanning for instant messages, comments or posts—anything from anyone she didn't recognize. Anything that seemed remotely suspect. But she wasn't terribly active on either platform and there was nothing out of the ordinary. She even checked her friend requests—none—and new followers—again, none.

She slammed back into the chair and ran a hand through her hair.

Okay, not social media. What then? Email?

Her work email account was now frozen, her access terminated based on a warrant executed by Investigator Fisk. But that didn't apply to her personal email account. How someone she didn't know would obtain her private email address was a bit of a mystery. She didn't exactly hand it out. Although that was also true of her cell phone number and, if there was any credence to this theory, the person trying to reach her had somehow managed to get that number.

The more she thought about it, her personal email address and cell number really wouldn't be that difficult to track down. Her law firm knew them. People she had socialized with back in Tampa had them. They were listed on forms she would have filled out in various places: the gym, rewards programs, her bar association personal profile, court records, doctor and dentist records, mailing lists...

They're out there to find if someone is desperate enough.

She opened her inbox and started scanning. She went back a whole month, but found nothing. The same was true for the spam folder. She even opened the trash which held over a thousand emails she had discarded for one reason or another. She scrolled back through a full month of those too, stopping to read them in their entirety whenever she came across one from a sender she didn't recognize—a notice for an upcoming legal seminar, an ad for a clothing line, and the like. But nothing looked suspicious.

After twenty minutes, she leaned back in the chair, absent-mindedly chewing on a nail. Maybe this theory was a dead end. Maybe no one was trying to reach her. Her eyes drifted aimlessly over the kitchen space as she thought it through. No texts, no email, no snail mail either. Just a couple of bills and flyers. No notes. No strange...envelopes...

Quinn's eyes dropped to the flowers in the trash can. The ones sent by Simon. Simon, who had only ever once sent her flowers, and that had been three years ago at the beginning of their relationship. Simon, who had broken off that relationship in very clear, final terms.

With the hesitant gait of a detonation specialist approaching a suspected bomb, Quinn moved to the trash can and gingerly pulled out the bouquet. The roses were turning brown where they had been smushed, as were the hydrangea blooms. The envelope sat in the greenery where she had shoved it before tossing out the whole thing. Quinn withdrew it and pulled out the card.

> Quinn, I still love you.
> Please don't give up on me, Peaches.
> I miss our walks, reading together in the
> morning over coffee, our everything.
> Please call me.

A shockwave rolled through her. Something definitely wasn't right. Simon had never called her Peaches once in their entire relationship. And walks together? Reading over coffee? Nonexistent.

Someone else had sent this. Sent it as Simon to disguise whoever they were and whatever their true motives were, in case someone other than Quinn intercepted it. But the sender would have known she would realize it wasn't actually from Simon as soon as she read it. They were likely counting on it. And on her deciphering the deeper meaning behind the words.

But this is just a bunch of nonsense.

Was "Peaches" a clue? She didn't keep any peaches in the house, or any fruit for that matter thanks to her terrible shopping habits.

Or maybe the reference to walking? But walking where?

She didn't have a walking pattern except up and down the beach, which didn't suggest anything helpful.

She considered the line about "reading together over coffee." Given their schedules, she and Simon had rarely seen each other before noon. In Tampa her mornings had been spent on her balcony, just like they were here on her porch—alone, coffee in hand, reading her devotion...

Possibility ripped through her like lightning and in seconds she was out the back door, racing to the rocking chair where she sat nearly every morning, reading her devotion book, *Hope For Each Day,* by Billy Graham, and the side table where she kept it.

Holding the book by its spine, Quinn used her thumb to flip through the pages—until they stopped on their own on the passage for October 11. Tucked tightly in between the pages, crammed as close to the spine as possible and taped in place, was a thin, two-inch silver key, and with it, a folded note, on the outside of which was written:

DO NOT GO INSIDE
DO NOT READ THIS ALOUD
THEY ARE LISTENING

27

Quinn lowered herself into a rocking chair, keeping the book in her lap. Her head shot up as she scanned the beach. No one seemed to be watching. But according to this warning, someone was listening.

Her heart thrumming like an engine, she unfolded the handwritten note.

Dear Quinn,

I don't have much space to explain. You are in danger. I have a plan, and I slipped in when you stepped out. I'm waiting here for you to come back home so I can explain in person, but in case that does not go well, I've planted this for you to find later. I've been watching you for several days and know your routine. I'm sure you'll find it. But I had to tuck it toward the back so it wouldn't be noticeable, and just in case you miss it, I've arranged for the flowers to come tomorrow as a secondary precaution. I know it sounds crazy, but given their resources, this is the only way.

The people coming after you are more dangerous than

you can imagine. Do not underestimate them. If they've found me, it's only a matter of time before they start in on you. This key is to a private mailbox at The Mailbox Office in Columbus, GA. All the answers are there.

I'm sorry if we didn't get to meet. And I'm sorry for the role I played in hurting you. My hope is that you can stop this before anyone else gets hurt. Because I promise you they will stop at nothing to make sure their secrets stay secret.

Your house is likely bugged. Your phone and car tracked. Leave everything and go as soon as you find this. Take the contents of the box to the FBI as soon as you collect it.

I'm sorry.

The note was unsigned. Quinn looked up again, her gaze darting from side to side up and down the beach. There was no one on the boardwalk, and the few people on the sand still didn't seem to be paying her any attention.

She looked back at the note, her heart skipping a beat. She sucked in a breath waiting for the rhythm to reestablish, which it did with a disturbing, out-of-time thump.

This was behind all the craziness happening to her. This note and the key in her hand would literally unlock the secrets behind the mayhem. For reasons she couldn't possibly fathom, whoever left these needed *her* to have them so badly, needed *her* to retrieve whatever was in that mailbox so desperately, that he had apparently died trying to make that happen.

She had no idea why. But she was going to find out.

QUINN EMERGED from the brush along the south side of Highway 98, a mile east from her house and about one hundred yards from The Little Red Shed. It was only a twenty-minute walk from her house to this point, not exactly strenuous, but dodging between houses and trudging through the sand dunes had left her huffing. After checking for anyone tailing her and seeing no one, she ran across Highway 98 to the north side and kept going.

Her plan was to approach The Little Red Shed from the rear, in case anyone was watching. She had left her phone and truck at home, so that if they were being tracked—as the author of the note suggested—it would appear she was still there. But she couldn't be sure someone wasn't keeping surveillance on her house from the beach side. If they saw her go, she hoped by now she had lost them in the growing dark.

She went one block farther north into a neighborhood, then cut over, stopping when she finally reached a spot she thought would be directly behind The Shed's property. After cutting through yards and over more than one fence, she finally saw the lights of The Shed and turned on the speed.

It was nearly eight thirty now. Thankfully, the area behind The Shed was blanketed in deep shadow, its garden and walking paths lit only by the strings of lights wrapped around trees and bushes. Quinn could only pray that it would be enough to keep her hidden.

She sprinted to the back door to The Shed's kitchen, coming up on it so fast that she had to catch herself with outstretched palms to keep from slamming into it. She had to knock three times before Ian finally opened the door, his brow furrowed, his face alight with concern.

"Quinn? What are you—"

"Lock it behind me, okay?" Quinn asked, stepping past him, then whirling around as he complied. He turned to face her, his expression grim.

"What's wrong?" he asked, a dark shade to his voice.

She held his gaze. "Everything, Ian. Everything."

28

The journey from Seaglass Cove to Columbus was a four-hour trip over primarily state and U.S. highways, which despite being mostly four-lane roads, still passed through some long, undeveloped stretches of backcountry. Quinn and Ian had left The Shed in his Jeep right around nine p.m., after she frantically explained just enough of the situation for him to understand that she needed to go as soon as possible.

"I can't ask you to go with me," she had said, inches from him in the walk-in storage unit where they had gone for privacy, "but I need to borrow your truck. And your cell. According to this," she held up the note, "they may have bugged and tracked mine." She had shivered then and he quickly pulled her into him, rubbing his hands up and down her arms for warmth. The gesture was more comforting than he could have known, and it took everything for her not to crumple into his embrace at that moment. But breaking down was not an option. No matter how much she wanted to, or how much she believed he would carry the load for her if she let him. This was her problem, not his.

But he wasn't having it. Which is why, instead, he drove them both away from The Shed in his Jeep, headed for Columbus. Quinn put up a bit of a fight about it, but not much. The truth was, she wanted him along.

She spent most of the first hour explaining what she discovered and how she had discovered it, as Ian peppered her with questions. The more she talked, the more idiotic she felt over the fact that the answer had been in her house the whole time.

"It's been sitting in my house for days. Days! I can't believe I just threw the flowers in the trash without reading the card. I knew something was off. It isn't like him to send flowers, but I'm just so...so...done with him. I didn't want to hear anything he had to say."

"You can't beat yourself up over that. You didn't know. And if I'm honest, I think it's pretty great you just dumped them in the trash." Though he was staring straight ahead into the darkness before them, Quinn could sense he was appraising her in his peripheral vision, waiting for her reaction.

"You do?" she asked, nervous anticipation running down her spine.

He nodded. "You're done with him and you know it. That's so much better than pining away for someone. Makes it easier to move on with your life."

"Well," she hedged, "it isn't all Simon's fault. I hurt him by creating a horrible situation, even though he took it badly."

"Any guy that wouldn't stand by you given what you were going through at the time isn't worthy of you. So, I'll say again, I'm glad you're done with him."

She turned fully in her seat now, staring at him, feeling her admiration slip onto her face in the form of a smile. "You're big on loyalty, aren't you?"

He turned briefly to face her. In the glow of the dashboard she could see the line of thick, dark lashes along his eyelids. "Aren't you?" he said, his voice taking on that low, meaningful quality he had used the other night. He looked back at the road, his hands seeming to grip the wheel more tightly.

"Absolutely," Quinn answered, a palpable pull reaching straight from her center, drawing her to him—as if willing her to jump across the console and into his arms. Instead, she resolutely twisted forward in her seat and forced a change of subject. "So what do you think is in the mailbox?"

He sucked in a loud breath, releasing it slowly. She cut her eyes at him to find him glancing over at her again, his eyes narrowed in amused vexation before they returned to the road. He wagged his head almost imperceptibly, then started chiming in with his theories.

They spent another twenty minutes bouncing ideas around, trying to make sense of the note and why its author would choose to handle things in this bizarre way. Was it because of a murder? Or murders? Embezzlement? Secrets that would ruin someone? The possibilities were endless, but right now it was all speculation. "We're wasting our time," Quinn finally conceded. "Without more to go on, we're shooting in the dark."

"Look, why don't you get some sleep," he said. "We've got another two hours to go until we get to Columbus."

"No, you should sleep," she argued. "I can take a turn driving."

"At this rate, we'll make it by one. I'll park somewhere and sleep then. The mailbox place doesn't open until eight, right?"

This idea didn't sit well with her. "Doesn't seem fair that you do all the driving."

"I'm a cop. Or at least I used to be. I'm used to working the night shift."

"Is that what you used to do? Work the night shift?" she asked, quickly snatching up the breadcrumb of his past he had dropped, likely an inadvertent slip on his part.

He rolled his lips inward and she could tell he was debating

Liar Like Her

whether to elaborate. "How about you stop wasting good sleep time and crawl in the back seat," he said.

Decided against sharing, then, she thought, disappointment pricking her gut. *When will he finally feel comfortable trusting me with whatever he's holding back? Is he afraid it'll change my opinion of him?*

As she unbuckled and dropped into the back seat, re-buckling before lying down, she couldn't imagine Ian Wolfe telling her anything that would make her think less of him.

After all, whatever his story was, the man in the car with her now was a good one. Whatever his story, she knew what it was like to need a fresh start. If he needed one, she would be the first to offer it.

173

29

Almost forty minutes had passed since Quinn crawled in the back, and Ian could hear her snoring gently.

Good. She needs the rest, he thought.

Now near midnight, traffic was sparse, headlights in the opposite direction only cutting the blackness sporadically as he rolled along in the quiet. He kept the radio off. He liked the silence. Made it easier to think.

And there was a lot to think about.

He still hadn't told her. A knot twisted in his stomach at the thought of it and the chance he passed up earlier, when she asked about his shifts on the job. It was the perfect opening to finally lay his past bare. But instead he watched it go by like the lines on the highway and kept his mouth shut.

Of course, she never would have asked about it had he not brought it up, and he mentally kicked himself for that. It wasn't like him to slip up, and it was a sure sign he was letting his guard down with Quinn.

But was that a good thing or a bad one?

Ever since he left that world behind, he had maintained a strict silence about his work on the force and the events that haunted him, finding it easier to pretend that nothing had happened at all. Easier to just start over from scratch, which led to his rule about not dating for now. Dating meant complications. It meant having to explain.

But Quinn Bello had come along and changed everything. Not only was he considering breaking his rule, he was also making the kind of mistakes he hadn't made even once since arriving in Seaglass Cove. Almost as if, deep down, he *wanted* her to know.

But the risk is so high.

If she knew, she might just walk away from him.

Or she might feel a kinship. If anyone would understand, it would be her.

He adjusted the rearview mirror downward, allowing him to see her beautiful face in the muted colors of night—slender nose, long eyelashes brushed toward her cheekbones, lips parted slightly—and her red hair piled around her, a devastating contrast against her fair skin. He exhaled a tight breath and returned the mirror to its proper position.

The bottom line was, he would never be able to guess ahead of time how she would react if he came clean. And until he came clean...well...she would never really know *him.*

It boiled down to this: Was being truly known by her something he wanted badly enough to risk losing her altogether?

30

Quinn propped her head up on one elbow, digging it into the cushion of the back seat. She lay on her side as she watched Ian sleeping in the driver's seat. It was nearly six thirty, and she woke ten minutes earlier to find he had parked the Jeep in a Costco parking lot somewhere in Columbus. She wasn't sure exactly where, as she didn't have her phone on her—she had left it in her house—and Ian's was clutched tightly in his right hand. But a billboard for "Prime Plumbers, the best in Columbus," at least clued her in to the fact that they had reached their destination.

She frowned, feeling guilty. He could have slept in the cargo area. There was plenty of room back there, but he chose to sleep sitting up in the driver's seat. On guard.

Probably something to do with his police instincts. Remaining in a position to act quickly if needed.

"Thank you, Lord, for him," she whispered, acutely aware that having Ian come into her life when he did was more of a blessing than she initially realized. He had plunged into the thick of this with her without a second thought, refusing to let her tackle it alone. She could have done it alone if she was forced to, but she was so glad that wasn't the case. Gratitude welled up, wetness brimming along her lower lids.

With a groan, he shifted, exposing the pistol tucked into the waistband of his pants. She had seen him retrieve it from underneath the counter at The Shed before they left, but didn't say anything. Given his former career, he obviously knew about weapons and how to assess risk. If he felt they were safer with it, she wouldn't argue. Unbidden, the memory of the corpse on the floor flashed in her mind, the smells and sights of that night rushing back as if she were there, sending a ripple of anxiety through her.

If Ian thought they needed a weapon, he probably wasn't wrong.

He stirred again, this time rolling his neck and stretching his arms. He yawned, turning in his seat toward her, then flashing a thousand-watt grin. "How long have you been awake?" he asked.

"Not long. You slept up front," she said, matter-of-factly stating the obvious.

Concern flitted across his face and he tensed. "Well, I thought we were pretty safe and that it was okay to get some rest." He sounded apologetic. "I didn't notice anyone tailing us and no one came along after I parked so I thought we would be fine. I'm sorry if I left you feeling vulnerable—"

"No, no, I wasn't second-guessing you! I just meant...that couldn't have been comfortable, sleeping up there. You could have taken the cargo area."

"Oh," he said, the muscles in his face and neck relaxing. "it wasn't a problem. And this way I could react faster—drive off quickly if I needed to. But how are you? You were snoring a bit," he said, more than a hint of teasing in his voice, "so I'm guessing you got some decent rest."

"Snoring, huh?" Hating that he actually heard that, she pushed herself into a seated position, rolling her shoulders, working out the kinks. "Well, now you really do know all my dirty little secrets," she joked, wrinkling her nose. "But, yeah, I feel fairly rested, considering. And very ready to see what's in that mailbox."

Ian lifted his hand from where he had been rubbing the base of his neck and pointed to the right. "The place is only a couple of streets over that way. Didn't want to park too close. Just in case."

"Well, we've got more than an hour, and I don't know about you, but I'm starving."

"I could eat," he said, patting his stomach.

"Good," she replied, poking one leg over the console after the other and dropping into the passenger seat. "But it's my turn to pay."

"Yes, ma'am, it is," he agreed enthusiastically.

"All right, then. Where's the nearest Hardees? Order anything you want. Sky's the limit."

THE MAILBOX OFFICE occupied one of a dozen units in a red-brick strip mall situated on a busy downtown street. It opened at 8:00 a.m., and after several minutes of watching to make sure no one was scouting the place, Ian and Quinn pushed through the front door at 8:10, feverish anticipation driving her steps.

An electronic chime announced their entry, but the clerk behind the counter—already busy helping another person mail a large box—barely looked up. Quinn tossed the clerk a quick smile and nod, and without slowing down headed straight for the wall of mailboxes to the right of the counter, looking for "126," the number printed on the key. She scanned the rows of small, brass-colored doors, her eyes racing over the number plates as a buzz began to build in her head.

There it is.

Box 126. Third row. Tenth box over. She dropped to a squat, her hand shooting out to touch the door at the same time Ian's did. His fingers were warm and solid and when she looked at him she could tell from his expression that she wasn't the only one feeling the spark the contact ignited.

"Key," she mumbled, holding his gaze as she pulled it from the pocket of her jeans with her free hand and brought it up to eye level.

"Key," he said, dropping his hand but not breaking his focus on her.

She inserted the key into the lock, turned it and pulled the door open. Inside was a thick manila envelope, folded into a "U-shape" to fit within the confines of the small mailbox. Quinn snatched it out, then peered inside the box to make sure there was nothing else.

Empty.

She shut the door and they stood simultaneously. The envelope was about an inch thick when unfolded. The recipient was listed as Brad Atkins, Box 126, 19 Grapple Avenue, Unit C, Columbus, GA 31906. The return address was the same.

"Come on," Ian said, pulling on Quinn's sleeve. "Let's not hang around." Nodding, she followed his lead, her pulse galloping like a racehorse as they hustled out the door.

31

"We're not sitting here while you read whatever's in there," Ian said, backing out of the space and pulling onto the main road as soon as traffic would allow. "You read, I'll drive," he said.

Quinn slid a finger across the envelope's flap, tearing it open and removing the contents. There was a letter to her and a clipped, thick stack of papers. She turned the envelope on its end, and a thumb drive and plastic identification card slid onto her lap.

She picked up the card. It was an employee photo identification badge for Rhinehardt Pharmaceuticals and, based on the strip on the back, also a keycard. The color photo on the front bore the name "Brad Atkins" and depicted a man in his late thirties with light-brown, wide-set eyes. Blonde-brown hair, cut short, no sideburns. A short, pudgy nose and thick brows that nearly touched.

Quinn's stomach flipped. "This is the dead man I found in my house." Though her hands were steady, the slight tremor in her voice betrayed her.

"Are you sure?"

"One hundred percent," she replied.

Ian made a hard right, then stepped on the gas, merging onto U.S. Highway 27 South, the road that would take them back to Seaglass Cove. "What's the letter say?"

The handwriting was the same as on the note hidden in her devotional book. After swallowing hard, Quinn read it aloud.

Dear Ms. Bello,

My name is Brad Atkins. You don't know me, but I know you. I've been trying to reach you for several weeks, but my attempts by telephone have failed. I can't leave a voicemail or email you, because while I'm not sure they will have been able to tap your phone, it's possible they've hacked it and/or your computer and will be able to access messages. So I'm coming to Seaglass Cove to see you. I don't think they'll realize I've left Raleigh until it's too late. I think I've managed to keep them from suspecting that I know what I know. At least I hope I have. Just in case, I mailed this before I left to safeguard it, in case something happens and I don't get to meet with you in person. You don't have a connection to Columbus, so they won't be looking for you there and it's pretty close to where you are, so it shouldn't be hard for you to make a quick trip.

I know this isn't making any sense. Please bear with me. It's a lot to explain.

I work for Rhinehardt Pharmaceuticals in Raleigh as a Junior Vice President of Research and Development. For the last twelve years we've been developing a new drug for the treatment of acute anxiety disorder—Anavexiam.

Nausea hammered Quinn and she gripped the paper tighter, her knuckles white. "Anavexiam. That's the new drug I started back in September when the alprazolam didn't work," she said, then continued reading.

I don't know what you know about the process of bringing a drug like that to market, but it's long and expensive and very risky. The last two drugs we were developing failed in the late stages of their clinical trials, at a loss of $200 million and $175 million, respectively. Rhinehardt spent $250 million preparing to bring Anavexiam to the public. In order to recover its losses from the earlier drug failures and not lose another $250 million on Anavexiam, the drug had to succeed.

Anavexiam received final approval nine months ago and we began marketing the drug immediately. The initial reports were very positive. But then there were problems.

In the third month after Anavexiam's release to the public, we learned of five problematic cases in different parts of the country involving Anavexiam patients who developed tragic and unexpected side effects. All of these patients had previously been prescribed a benzodiazepine —like alprazolam or clonazepam—to control their anxiety, without success. Their physicians switched them to Anavexiam to see if it would produce better results. You were one of these cases.

Unfortunately, in four of those cases, the patient committed suicide within 4-6 weeks of starting Anavexiam. According to their medical records, each patient had previously exhibited suicidal tendencies. Consequently, these cases did not raise red flags as the patients were already suicide prone.

Your case was different in that, although you did not attempt suicide after using Anavexiam, you did manifest paranoia and direct it at others with violent results. While you had no prior history of such paranoia or violence, it was also true that while you were taking Anavexiam you admitted to self-medicating with your discontinued alprazolam and alcohol. It was decided that this combination of over-medicating and alcohol usage, not the Anavexiam, resulted in your dangerously erratic behavior, and the case was treated as statistically insignificant.

However, several weeks ago I stumbled onto information that suggested a cover-up at the highest levels of Rhinehardt concerning these issues. I started digging and what I've uncovered proves it.

To start with, the fourth patient and his wife were killed when he supposedly drove their car off a bridge after leaving a suicide note at home. But I've found emails proving that just prior to his death he and his wife had begun to question the effect Anavexiam was having on his state of mind—including hallucinations and paranoia he had never experienced before. They voiced these concerns to his physician and to Rhinehardt through reporting channels, but nothing was done. I even suspect his physician may have been bribed to alter the patient's records to reflect a history of prior suicidal thoughts.

I continued gathering as much as I could from the inside, and I now believe the patient and his wife were killed to keep them quiet. Which leads me to think that patients 1-3 may not have committed suicide either. I believe you were only spared because your continued use of alcohol and alprazolam on top of the Anavexiam conveniently explained your behavior without specifically pointing a finger at Anavexiam.

Rhinehardt needs Anavexiam to remain viable and in the market to avoid crippling financial repercussions. Their pockets are deeper, and their influence more far-reaching than you can imagine. I now believe that they've done and paid whatever was necessary to keep the truth hidden and will continue to do so.

And it gets worse.

At first I believed Rhinehardt was just covering up problems which came to light after Anavexiam's release. But I have since discovered documentation proving that Rhinehardt became aware of the drug's potential danger during the Stage III clinical trials, but covered it up to keep the drug in line for approval. This means that Anavexiam isn't just a failed drug. It's a failed drug with potentially catastrophic side effects that Rhinehardt knowingly delivered to the market with a callous disregard for the outcome.

The data suggests that patients with certain pre-existing conditions may react negatively to Anavexiam, experiencing side effects of hallucinations, paranoia, excessive panic and irrational thought, becoming dangerous to themselves and others. The common factors in the five cases I've discussed are: you each experienced childhood seizures, currently experience migraines, and have heart palpitations (PVCs).

While it might be rare for a patient taking Anavexium to meet all these conditions, it can happen and it happened with the five of you, and apparently also with one or more patients in the Stage III clinical trials. If word got out about this lethal combination, it would ruin the drug. The FDA would pull it—at least until further studies (taking years) could be completed—and patients with any of these factors, and especially those with two or more of them, wouldn't want to take it anyway because of the risks. This would kill the drug, given the incredibly high number of people who experience both migraines and at least occasional PVCs.

Quinn sucked in air, her chest tightening as the words washed over her and she tried to absorb the meaning behind the information in the letter.

"Is that true? Do you have all those things?" Ian asked.

Quinn nodded. "The childhood seizures ended when I was

ten. I get migraines, usually with stress and weather changes. And yes, I have PVCs."

"What else does it say?" Ian asked, jerking his head toward the paper, his voice urgent. Quinn's gaze returned to the letter.

If they discover that I know the truth, I have no doubt they'll get rid of me. But my conscience won't allow me to remain silent. I'm coming to you first before going to the authorities for two reasons. One, you aren't safe and there isn't a moment to lose. I believe they're still watching you and that if you do anything or your condition takes a turn that jeopardizes this drug's viability, or if circumstances change, making your suicide somehow appear credible, I have no doubt they'll remove you from the picture. If I contact the authorities first, by the time they understand what's going on and that you need protection, you'll be dead. I need to bring you into this so we can immediately get you the protection you need, and make sure you understand what happened so you never take that drug again.

Second, you are the only survivor who experienced the side effects firsthand. What happened to you in Tampa was not the result of your anxiety condition or you losing control. Yes, you drank and double-dipped on meds, but Anavexiam produced the hallucinations and paranoia in you because of your pre-existing conditions, and it is responsible for causing you to do what you did. Basically, you were drugged. I need you to tell this story, your story, to the authorities, but we have to be careful because I don't know who to trust. Rhinehardt had to have help from someone on the inside of one or more agencies in order to hide the problems with Anavexium and secure its approval. I just don't know who.

I'm flying into Atlanta and driving down, in the hopes that if they are following me, I'll be able to lose them before they know where I'm headed. I want to bring you in, explain this to you in person—be sure you never use Anavexiam again—and together take this information to the right people to be investigated. You're a lawyer. You understand how that side of it works better than I do. We need each other.

If something happens and I don't make it to see you, be aware that they'll be watching your every move. Get away from Seaglass Cove and take these materials—there's also a thumb drive with files I was able to download and a video of me essentially explaining all this—to someone you decide you can trust in the FBI. If you've got personal contacts, use them. All the documents to prove what I've said in this letter are attached.

As a final precaution, I've uploaded the video and copies of this letter and the enclosed documents to an online email service. I've set a timer for its release to you, a news station in Raleigh, and the Atlanta FBI office—to an agent I essentially chose at random. I reset the timer every Thursday. If I meet with you, it'll never go out. But if I'm gone I have to put the information out there in order to protect the public. It's risky because if it does go out, Rhinehardt might come after you before you know what's happening. I'm sorry if that's the way this went down, because it will probably put you in more danger. But I can't die with no one knowing.

You're the key to undoing this, Quinn. You're the only one left alive to tell the story. I don't know if your doctor is involved, but with the kind of money Rhinehardt waves around, you can't rule it out so don't trust her. When you start asking questions, they'll do everything they can to discredit you, then silence you. Please be careful. Move quickly. Godspeed.

Brad Atkins

The letter ended with an email login and password for the service holding the electronic message that was queued to be sent if Atkins didn't reset the timer.

"You're gonna need to log on and reset that timer so those emails don't go out yet. Not until we've figured out what to do," Ian said. It was only Tuesday. They still had time. But he was right. They would need to reset it soon.

Quinn dropped the letter onto her lap, her hand shaking as she reached over to grip Ian's leg. He covered her hand with his and she could feel hot tears gathering as his sympathetic gaze swiveled to meet hers. "You know what this means?" she asked weakly.

Ian's lips formed a thin line as he nodded.

"It means I wasn't crazy. And it wasn't my fault." She barely got the last word out before a sob racked her. Lifting his hand from hers, he threw his arm around her and pulled her into his shoulder, hugging her tightly as she felt the waves of relief and anger and exhaustion come, pouring out in choked gasps. She pressed into him, breathing in his scent of sandalwood, focusing on that and striving to calm down, to hold it together and *breathe*. But it was too much. Surrendering to the surging tidal wave of emotion, she abandoned the attempt at composure and let it all go.

32

Quinn's mind spun as she tried to process the truths in the letter. A man was dead. A man named Brad Atkins whose conscience had compelled him to act. To seek her out. To protect her and others. And they had killed him for it.

Ian continued driving south on Highway 27 while they batted ideas back and forth about who to contact, who not to contact, and whether or not to go straight to Shane Cody and Investigator Fisk. Ian stepped on the gas, passing a logging truck, then swung back into the right lane. "There's my brother's friend—the special agent in the Florida Department of Law Enforcement—we could reach out to Jason," he said.

"I don't know. Atkins specified the FBI. Maybe we should stick to that," Quinn replied.

"Do you know anyone in the FBI?"

Quinn sighed, wagging her head. "I used to. Back when I started at the law firm in Tampa I knew a guy..." She trailed off. "But it's been years. He'd probably be safe though." Disquiet bubbled within her. "But why the FBI? Why not the FDA?

They're the ones who govern the approval process. Wouldn't that be where we should start?"

"Atkins said Rhinehardt was paying people off. It would make sense for one of them to be inside the FDA. If you reach out to the wrong person, you could end up like those other patients. I say we drive straight to Tallahassee. Go to my brother's house and figure this out. Ten-to-one his buddy can get us in front of an FBI agent quicker than we could on our own."

She didn't like dragging Ian's brother into this thing. But at the moment she didn't see another option. "I think you may be right. I definitely don't think I can go back to Seaglass Cove. Not if they're watching my house. By now they probably know I'm gone." It was an easy enough drive to Tallahassee, as Highway 27 ran right through it. *Maybe it's a sign,* Quinn thought.

"So Tallahassee it is," Ian said.

"But I don't want to go to your brother's house," she said, qualifying her agreement to his plan. "I don't want to endanger him. We'll find a hotel somewhere."

Ian nodded. "Okay, yeah. That's smart."

"And...Ian, are you sure? I mean, I don't want you to feel obligated. I know you came this far, but you didn't know what you were getting into."

Ian's eyes flicked to the rearview mirror, then he stepped on the brakes, slowing the Jeep smoothly but quickly. He veered onto the shoulder, bringing them to a stop, dust swirling behind the SUV. They were in the middle of no-man's-land— no towns, no businesses, just woods, creeks, and county highways.

She swiveled toward him, confused. "What are you—"

He twisted in his seat, his eyes full of purpose as he interrupted, "No, I didn't know what I was getting into." He leaned in, closing the space between them, cupping her face in his hands. "I just knew it didn't matter."

And then he kissed her, and there was only dizziness and Ian and warmth and more feeling, more hope...*just more.* Finally he pulled back from her, threading the fingers of one hand through the red locks draped over her shoulder. His charcoal eyes met her gaze with unabashed intensity. "I'm in this thing. End of story."

She dropped her forehead against his, closing her eyes. "Okay."

He kissed her again, sending waves of electricity through her until, with a heavy sigh, he leaned back in his seat, put the Jeep into gear and pulled onto the highway. He laid his open hand on the center console and she reached for it, intertwining their fingers. Though her spirit lifted at his touch, a hard knot was forming in her gut. One she couldn't ignore.

"There's something I need to talk to you about," she said softly.

"Shoot." His voice was relaxed, but his grip on her hand tightened almost imperceptibly, as if she had triggered some measure of apprehension that involuntarily forced the contraction.

"What's your relationship with Meghan Carne?" she asked.

Ian turned to look at her, puzzlement knitting his eyebrows together. "Meghan Carne?"

"I've seen the two of you...interacting...at The Shed a few times. I thought maybe there was something there."

"No," Ian answered emphatically. "Absolutely not."

Quinn's stomach knot began to unravel. "It just seemed like you were pretty chummy."

"Meghan's the one who's chummy. She's also chummy with every guy that walks in there. It's just easier to let her be. But she's not my type."

The corner of Quinn's mouth drew up. "Really? And what's your type?"

Without skipping a beat Ian flipped down Quinn's sun visor, opened the vanity mirror on the back, and tapped it.

Quinn snorted. "Smooth."

"Glad to see you're finally getting that." A confident grin played on his face, but after a few seconds it seemed to lose its vitality.

He cut a sideways glance at her, then fixed his gaze back on the road. "But speaking of things we need to talk about, I think maybe it's time I come clean about something."

C ool air blew from the vents, tickling Quinn's face and sending strands of hair fluttering above her shoulders. The greasy scent of the sausage biscuits from that morning still lingered, the takeout bag crumpled on the floorboard at her feet. The radio was off and there was only the sound of the road whirring beneath them and Ian's somber voice.

"I don't like to talk about it," he started, his fingers now gripping hard at ten and two on the steering wheel. "I came to Seaglass Cove to start over, and I thought it would be easier if people didn't know my story. But it doesn't feel right holding back from you anymore."

"Okay," Quinn said, a nervous noose tightening around her chest as she wondered whether this was going to be something she really wanted to know.

"I joined the Chicago P.D. right after I graduated from Northwestern with a degree in criminal justice. I always knew I wanted to be a cop, but Dad insisted I go to college first. As soon as I could I applied to be a detective, and by the time I was twenty-seven I was assigned to the Bureau of Organized Crime, Narcotics Division."

"That sounds dangerous," she said.

"Sometimes. But I was good at it. Kept catching bigger cases, moving up in the pecking order. I had some good friends there and we accomplished a lot. Got a lot of dangerous stuff and people off the streets. Saved lives."

There was something about the hollow way he was speaking that made Quinn think Ian wasn't telling *her* this, so much as he was telling himself—something she suspected he had done many times. She waited silently, not pushing, giving him space until finally he started up again.

"Our unit saw a lot of seized narcotics pass through it. Narcotics worth a lot of money. The kind of money a cop could work his whole career and never see. At some point some of the guys in my division—a few of the other detectives—decided to start skimming from the evidence. I didn't know about it," he said quickly, glancing over at her for the first time since he started explaining. "It was a group who came in about ten years before me. Eventually I started to have a bad feeling about things. A little voice nagging me that something wasn't right."

"Why?" she asked.

"I don't know. Little things that didn't add up. A discrepancy here and there—always explained of course."

"What did you do?"

"That's just it. I did nothing," he replied. "I made a choice to trust them, even though I had my doubts. These were guys that, by that time, I'd worked with for over four years. They had taken me in. Looked out for me. Even saved my life a couple of times. So I shoved my misgivings away and took them at their word. It was just easier.

"And then it all blew up. Someone else in the department had suspicions which prompted an undercover investigation. All three of the guys involved were brought down. I had to fight hard to prove I wasn't a part of it because I was so close to them." He sniffed. "One of them was my partner. They all confirmed I knew nothing about it, but eventually it came out that I'd had my suspicions along the way and hadn't done anything. They offered me a choice. Resign or be fired for negligent performance of duties. So I resigned." Though he was facing straight ahead, Quinn could see a glistening at the edge of his eye, and her heart melted.

"Ian, I'm so sorry."

He shook his head. "Thing is, I had it coming. Yeah, I trusted those guys and yeah, they lied to me, but somewhere deep down I knew the truth. I just didn't want to face it. I went against my better instincts—what I knew was right, who I really am—because it was the path of least resistance. And I had to pay the price."

He drew in a long, deep breath, Quinn silent as she extended a hand back across the center console. He dropped his right hand from the wheel and clasped hers, holding on to it as if it anchored him. "I kept my mouth shut when I should have spoken out. I chose poorly. Instead of standing strong and stepping out, I took the easy route because I was scared to rock the boat. Scared of what I might lose if I blew the whistle. Turned out I lost anyway—my credibility, my job, my reputation. Friends too, and my faith in myself."

He stole a quick glance at her. "When you talk about labels, about mistakes that define you and feeling like you're just resigned to be what everyone thinks of you...I get it. I *really* do. And wanting someone to believe in you without reservation? I get that too. I think that's part of what drew me to you. I recognized the same brokenness in you that's in me. I wasn't looking for someone to get involved with, Quinn. When I resigned from the force, Dad happened to be moving into his facility at the same time. So, I thought—perfect timing. I'll disappear into some tiny town near him, cook for people—the only other thing I'm good at—and start a new life. I made it a rule to keep to myself, stay out of trouble and out of other people's lives. And especially to avoid romantic entanglements.

"But then you walked in The Shed the morning after the break-in...I mean I've always thought you were...well, attractive...but that day I saw a kindred spirit and I just wanted to make it right. Because I wish somebody could have made it right for me. I know what it's like to need a second chance. I want to be yours. If what I just told you hasn't completely put you off me."

Overwhelming affinity gushed up within Quinn and she squeezed his hand, then leaned into him, putting her head on his shoulder. "Like you said, if anyone understands needing a second chance, it's me. And what was it you told me? Your mistake isn't who you are. It's just one bad choice you made."

"You haven't felt that way about yourself, though."

"No, but this," she said, pointing to the manila envelope beside her in the seat, "this really could change things."

"When it all comes out, you'll get your life back, including your law license. And people will understand now. They won't judge you the same way."

"The license, yes. But change people's estimation of me? I don't know if I can shake the old labels at this point."

"God didn't make people *things* to be labeled by their mistakes. He made them souls to grow from them. Your mistakes were part of your growing process. They played a role in your becoming, but they aren't what you've become. You're more than a label. You've got to decide once and for all who *you* believe yourself to be. You have faith. Does that faith say your identity is defined by your past, or by the God who rescued you and who he says you are? Until you decide that, you won't have peace."

"What if I can't find peace in Seaglass Cove with the history I have there?"

"You don't have to stay in Seaglass Cove. I get it if you can't. You shouldn't have to live in a place where you're fighting unfair prejudices constantly. But you also need to realize that wherever you go, there will always be that moment when someone is going to misunderstand you, or your intentions, or judge you. The only way to have peace through it all is to know in your heart who you are." He slowed the Jeep and pointed to a sign announcing a gas station half a mile up. "We're low on gas," he said. "I'm just gonna stop real quick."

Is he right? Quinn thought. *Is this more of a heart issue than a geographic one?* "So you think I should stay in Seaglass Cove? Tough it out?"

"I'm saying 'toughing it out' is the wrong strategy. You've been toughing it out for too long. And it isn't just other people's opinions that created the situation. I think, because of your guilt, you've voluntarily been carrying these negative labels since the night your friends took that boat out. You've lived your whole life trying to disprove them, when what you really need to do is rip the labels off and refuse to claim them anymore."

"And if others won't let me?"

"Let you? Quinn, you can't control how others perceive you. If you're waiting for someone else to come along and rip the labels off for you, you're wasting your time. You have to do it yourself. And if someone tries to slap one back on you, you have to choose not to accept it. Let it bounce off of you instead of torment you."

"I'm rubber and you're glue?" she said, a smile lifting her mouth.

He chuckled. "I guess so."

Ian took a right turn off the highway, then a quick left onto the access road leading to the gas station about a hundred yards down. But as they rolled along, something remained unsettled deep in Quinn's core. Something Ian said earlier about him relating to her brokenness. She ran her thumb over his hand, contemplating the best way to ask about it. She landed on being straightforward. "But...I'm not just some charity case you want to save, right?"

Ian turned to look at her, the Jeep now bouncing intermittently on the pothole-filled road. "Are you kidding me?"

She wasn't. She wanted this, but not if it was built on the wrong reasons. She held his gaze, and gave the tiniest twitch of her head.

He tightened his grip on her hand as he resumed looking straight ahead. "What we have in common may be part of why I was drawn to you, but it wasn't the only reason. And it wasn't what kept me coming back. *You* are. All of you."

She grinned, relief pouring into her. "I'm really glad—"

A violent impact at the back of the Jeep slammed Quinn forward, her seat belt yanking hard against her. Ian whipped forward too, but managed to slam on the brakes, bringing them to a screeching halt.

"You okay?" he asked, grasping her shoulder. The usually faint lines in his forehead were etched deeper, concern sharp in his gaze.

She nodded, sucking in a breath. "Yeah, I'm—"

Ian's eyes went wide at the same time there was a hard rap on Quinn's window. She swiveled to see a man standing outside her door, holding a gun aimed at her chest.

34

Three men were in the car that rear-ended them. What was made to seem like a fender-bender was actually a targeted kidnapping. The men forced Ian and Quinn into the back seat of Ian's Jeep—after patting them down and removing Ian's weapon—then drove to a secluded spot on a country road. They bound their hands with zip-ties, then moved them into the Jeep's cargo area, instructing them to shut up, lie down and stay down. One drove off in the car that had hit them, leaving the other two to take the Jeep—one driving and one in the back seat holding a weapon on Ian and Quinn during the entire trip back to Seaglass Cove.

There were no explanations given. Only silence and fear and the foreboding fact that their captors weren't wearing masks and she and Ian had not been blindfolded. It meant the men weren't worried about being identified later.

Just north of Seaglass Cove, in another remote spot, they pulled Quinn and Ian out of the Jeep. They cut the zip-ties on Ian and put him in the driver's seat, then put Quinn, still bound, in the front passenger seat. They instructed Ian to drive to his house while they hid on the back seat floorboard, threatening to shoot Quinn if Ian tried anything. Ian complied, driving to his small, ranch-style house on the east side of town, pulling into his garage and lowering the door as instructed. The men ordered Ian and Quinn into the living room, then onto the couch where they now sat side by side, Ian protectively sidled up against Quinn, his body slightly angled in front of her, his hands zip-tied again.

Of the two men, the one who seemed to be in charge was older, maybe in his early forties, with dark-brown hair, a sharp chin and eyes devoid of feeling. The other man, a late twenty-something, had a buzz cut, a weightlifter's build and rarely spoke. The older one took a ladder-back chair from the kitchen table, spun it around backward and sat down, the gun in his hand hanging over the top rung. The younger man stood behind him, poised to act if needed.

"You finally going to explain what's going on?" Ian asked, his words harsh.

Older Guy glowered at Ian but said nothing, then turned his attention to Quinn. "We need to know what you know," he demanded, his cold stare fixed on her.

"I don't know anything," she said, working hard to keep her voice steady despite the fear that had been flowing through her veins since the men shoved them in the back of the Jeep. "Honestly! Just what's on those pages," she said, nodding toward Atkins's manila envelope now held by Younger Guy.

"There's more you're not telling us," Older Guy said.

"There's not," Quinn said, her voice thin, nearly cracking.

"Do you think I'm stupid, Ms. Bello?" Older Guy asked, his expression darkening by the second.

"No, I don't—"

He cut her off by sucking in a long breath, then exhaling. "You think I can't get the answers I want from you? Just look at what we've done to you. To your reputation. To your freedom. We have resources you can't comprehend. Trying to hold out on us is a waste of time. We *will* get answers." In his guttural tone, he practically growled the word "will," like a sinister promise Quinn did not doubt he would keep.

"You don't have to do this, capiche?" Ian piped in, the same undertone of authority in his voice that he had used with Shane when standing in Quinn's foyer just nights ago.

Older Guy raised one eyebrow, though he did not appear amused. "*Capiche*? Seriously?" He pointed at Ian. "You, keep your mouth shut. And you," he said, now angling his finger at Quinn, "start talking."

"I don't have anything else to tell you," she said.

He groaned. "Look, I'm tired. I've been in this nowhere town for six weeks, watching you, waiting for something to happen. I'm ready to be out of here. And I can promise you're gonna hate this a lot less if you just spill it, starting with what happened at your house last night that made you head to Columbus—yeah, we were watching you. Nice touch, by the way, leaving your phone and truck behind—"

"So that's how you knew Atkins was there that night," Ian blurted, drawing the gazes of both men. "And I'll bet you had the place bugged for weeks. That's how you intercepted him before he could talk to Quinn."

"Aren't you brilliant, *Detective*," Older Guy quipped.

"Pretty lucky getting that body out of her house before the cops got there, though," Ian said. "Otherwise—"

"Luck had nothin' to do with it," barked Younger Guy, scowling as he stepped toward Ian.

Older Guy put a hand out, holding Younger Guy back.

"You got lucky," Ian taunted.

What is he doing? Quinn thought, fighting the urge to throw Ian a look warning him to stop antagonizing them. It wasn't helping.

"No, what we had was weeks of intel on Atkins, and the

upper hand when the little rat pulled a knife on my partner here," Younger Guy said, throwing back his shoulders.

"It doesn't matter," Older Guy chimed in. "What does matter is that when you left on foot last night, we followed, and as expected you went straight to your knight-in-shining-armor," he said, inclining his head toward Ian, "where we popped a tracker on his truck. Columbus was a surprise, but the minute you two went in that mailbox office, we bugged the Jeep then sat back and waited. You got in the truck, read Atkins's letter out loud and told us *almost* everything we needed to know. So now, what I need you to tell me—what we don't know—is, what sent you running to Columbus?" He narrowed his gaze. "It's important we have that information. You know, loose ends, and all that."

When she didn't immediately respond, he jerked his chair forward, putting his face only a foot from hers. She could see the malevolence simmering in his eyes. He would hurt her if he had to.

Still, she clamped her lips together. She wasn't going to make it easy for them. And if she dragged it on, maybe they could figure a way out of this. Get help. Stalling was her only weapon at this point.

But Older Guy wasn't having it. He sighed, then lowered his gun so that the barrel rested on Quinn's knee. "What made you take off last night?"

Quinn's insides turned to ice as the weight of the gun pressed against her. As she uttered a silent prayer for help, for wisdom, Ian spoke.

"Quinn, tell them," he said, nodding encouragingly. "You don't want him to hurt you."

"He's right. You don't want that," Older Guy said.

She exhaled a staggered breath, then explained about the flowers and card from Atkins, as well as the letter and key he left her.

Older Guy snickered appreciatively. "The *flowers*. Not that we didn't check with the florist," he added, as if defending himself and his skill set, "but it checked out as being ordered by your ex." He squinted at her. "And that's everything?"

She nodded. "That's everything. Really."

He sucked in a breath. "You know," he said, waving the barrel of the gun back and forth between them, you'd have been fine if Atkins hadn't dragged you into this. It's too bad he got a conscience about the whole thing."

"How can you *not* have one?" Quinn spat, unable to hold her tongue despite her fear. "You've killed people to keep the dangers of this drug quiet, to keep it out there even though no one knows how many more will suffer."

"That drug is money, and money makes the world go 'round," Older Guy said, then lifted his empty hand into the space above his head. Younger Guy laid Atkins's manila envelope into it. "This is the last piece of the puzzle we needed. The timed email Atkins mentions in here isn't an issue. He did a decent job, but we found that account a few days ago. Now all that's left is you."

Panic revved like an engine inside her, sending Quinn's mind scrambling for something to delay the inevitable, but it was Ian who spoke. "If you get rid of us, the authorities will know something's up. They'll finally have a reason to believe Quinn about the body and everything else and they'll start digging."

"No, they won't. We've set her up to look like a woman on the edge, paranoid again, losing control—the vandalism, all the planted evidence, nasty emails to the people who owned the house *we* burned down—they think she's losing it." He turned his frigid stare on Quinn, sending a shiver through her. "Honestly when you walked in on Atkins's body before we had a chance to drag him out of there, I thought it was over. But in the end your story just made you seem more nuts." He sighed. "So here's what's going to happen," he said, shaking the gun at Quinn. "You're gonna write a note explaining that you were falling for him," he waved the gun at Ian, "but suspected he was into someone else. Cheating on you."

"That's ridiculous. No one will buy that," Quinn said, her voice breathy. She felt weak, and her heart skipped one beat, then another.

"They will. Because you're paranoid. Drinking again. Fighting with neighbors and vandalizing their cars. You're one step away from being arrested for arson. This'll just be the nail in the coffin. Literally."

"Well, not literally," Ian said. "There's no coffin, no nail—"

Shocked by his nervy retort, Quinn's head snapped to Ian at the same time Younger Guy stepped over and popped him on the side of the head. Desperate to distract them from hurting Ian further, she blurted, "I'm not writing a suicide note." And she meant it. The thought of being complicit in furthering more lies about herself, about leaving that as her last act, was too sickening to comprehend.

Older Guy leaned in. "This is happening one way or another."

"You do anything to me, they'll know it wasn't a suicide," she said, straightening up and trying to appear braver than she felt.

"True," Older Man admitted, then nodded at Younger Guy, who put his gun against Ian's temple. "If you don't cooperate, we'll just make it look like you were really, *really,* angry when you confronted your boyfriend, here. They'll need dental records to identify him."

The hopelessness of their situation drove a wave of light-headedness through Quinn so severe that little lights began popping in her vision. She looked over at Ian, and felt a tear tracking down her cheek as he smiled sadly at her, squeezing her leg.

"It'll be okay," he said.

But it won't be.

Older Guy went into the kitchen and after a minute of digging around, came back with a pen and an unopened piece of junk mail. He handed them to Quinn. "Start writing exactly what I tell you."

～

IT TOOK LESS than five minutes for Older Guy to dictate the murder-suicide note to Quinn. Every stroke of the pen carved a deeper wound in her heart. Not only because of her regret for bringing Ian into this, but also because this final, irrevocable lie would be the thing she was most remembered for. As she signed her name with the zip-tie around her wrists boring into her skin, tears dotted the paper, smearing the ink.

"Give me that," Older Guy said, grabbing the envelope from Quinn and reading it. "Looks good," he muttered, then placed it on the kitchen counter where it would be seen by anyone who might come in later.

And find us here. Dead, she thought.

Older Guy eyed them both, no pity in his gaze. "Let's finish this."

While Older Guy kept a gun trained on the two of them, Younger Guy ransacked the room—shoving papers to the floor, knocking plants over, turning a table on its side—clearly staging the aftermath of a struggle. Quinn shuddered, her brain buzzing with the knowledge of what was coming. "I'm so sorry, Ian," she whispered, leaning against him, pressing her weight into his side in an effort to both comfort and be comforted.

His eyes were deep pools of grey, holding hers, willing her to stay strong. "It's okay, Quinn. It'll be okay. I promise."

"I'm so sorry," she repeated, feeling as if her soul were being rent in two. "You shouldn't even be here—"

204

The front door of the house burst open, slamming against the wall, as multiple sheriff's deputies swarmed inside.

"Freeze!"

"Weapons down, weapons down!"

"Drop it! Get on the floor!"

Both men dropped their guns, the sound of the weapons clattering onto the hardwoods lost in the noise of the chaos, as they lay face-down on the floor and were surrounded by deputies. Simultaneously, Ian and Quinn raised their bound hands into the air above their heads, as a deputy approached them and ordered them to remain where they were. Relief rushed up in Quinn, escaping in a choked cry as Ian expelled a loud whoosh of breath. She turned to see him red-faced, a line of moisture gathering along his lower eyelids.

"I wasn't sure that was going to work," he said, now counter-leaning his weight against Quinn, apparently finally giving in to his own emotional fatigue.

"That what was going to work?" she asked over the multiple shouts of "clear" coming from all corners of the house.

Before Ian could answer, Shane Cody raced up to them, holstering his weapon as he knelt in front of Quinn. "Are you all right?" he asked, his voice grave.

Quinn nodded, her limbs beginning to tremble in the aftershock. "We're fine. But I don't understand...how did you know?"

"We'll get to that," Shane said, "but first I need you to bring me up to speed."

IT TOOK the better part of an hour to walk Shane and Investigator Fisk through the events of the last eighteen hours, including Brad Atkins's note from the devotional book and the contents of the manila envelope. Most of the documentation he had provided would require industry experts to make sense of it. But the truth was obvious. Quinn had been set up to hide secrets that, if exposed, would cost Rhinehardt Pharmaceuticals hundreds of millions.

"I am so, so sorry, Quinn," Shane said as he sat with Quinn, Ian, and Fisk in Ian's living room. He rubbed a hand over his head, the lines in his face deep as he spoke. "I should have believed you."

Yeah, you should have, was what Quinn wanted to say. But she didn't. Right now, she was feeling pretty generous with her forgiveness.

"It's okay. I get it, Shane. You weren't the only one." At this, Fisk shifted uncomfortably in his seat. "I'm just glad the truth's finally out," she said. As she looked at him, her unanswered question from earlier flashed in her mind. "You never said how you knew to come here, though." Her head snapped to Ian, as she also remembered the unanswered question she had posed to him. "And what did you mean, that you 'didn't think it would work'?"

A satisfied expression washed over Ian's face. "You remember me telling you the other night that the *Riki* device can do some pretty cool things?"

"You said it told jokes," Quinn replied.

"Well, that's one of the things it can do. A while back I downloaded an app onto *Riki* designed to call 9-1-1 when it hears a preset trigger phrase. It makes the call silently, provides the address to the operator, then records whatever it hears for the next thirty minutes, sending it straight to the operator as if it's the other end of a phone call. It's like a personal bat signal."

Quinn's mind flashed through Ian's antagonizing exchanges with their kidnappers. One phrase stuck out, and when she thought of it, her mouth dropped open. "It was that weird thing you said, wasn't it? 'Don't do this, capi—'" Ian's hand shot out, covering Quinn's mouth before she could finish.

"Stop," he said, a soft chuckle escaping, "or it'll call 9-1-1 again. That's not exactly the phrase, but it's pretty close. Let's not test *Riki's* accuracy, okay?"

"What would make you think to set that up?" she asked.

"Retired cop, remember?"

"But that phrase—"

"It had to be something no one would ever say accidentally, but something I could work in if someone ever broke into the place and got the drop on me."

Finally she understood why he had been so belligerent with the kidnappers. "All those times you were egging them on— you were stalling?"

Ian nodded, his gaze falling on Shane. "It only took you guys fifteen minutes after I triggered it. I'm impressed."

Investigator Fisk nodded, as if accepting the compliment, but Shane leaned forward, bracing his forearms against his thighs, his hands folded as he directed himself to Quinn.

"And so the drug...that's responsible for what happened to you in Tampa?" he asked, his voice soft, almost timid. "So, in the courtroom—that wasn't you?"

She shook her head. "It wasn't me."

Shane inhaled a deep breath, then sat up. "Quinn, I really hope that when all this comes out it'll be enough to set the record straight. And enough for you to get your life back."

Quinn looked at Ian, who reached over and firmly took her hand. He interlaced his fingers with hers and the depth of feeling that welled up in her was something she knew she never wanted to be without. "Well, it should be enough to get my law license back. But," she continued, the corners of her mouth pulling up into a grin, "as for my life...that's in Seaglass Cove now."

35

Six Months Later

A November more mild than most was blessing Seaglass Cove, keeping temperatures around seventy degrees with almost no humidity and so far, no hurricanes. After stopping by to say a quick goodbye to Lena in the office down the hall, at nearly two p.m. Quinn walked out of the new offices of the Hope Community Legal Assistance Center with her briefcase full and her heart excited for the Saturday paddling adventure awaiting her.

As she drove her pickup down the road, she held one arm out the window, her hand gliding along in the wind, her fingers dancing in it. It had taken three months for the Florida Bar Association to reinstate her license and she had spent the first half of that trying to decide what she wanted to do once she got her license back. The second half she spent establishing the Hope Community Legal Assistance Center as part of the Hope Community Center. Lena had been on board from day one. Quinn did the work completely on a volunteer basis. It paid nothing, there was no opportunity for advancement, and absolutely, positively no perks. At least not the material kind.

She still held the position of manager of Bello Realty—she enjoyed that too, and after all, she had to pay the bills. And she was good at it, something her parents witnessed firsthand when they had come to visit. Quinn smiled at the thought of how happy it had made them to see her settled into a rhythm and fulfilled in her job and life in general. It had been a long time since they witnessed that.

But as often as her realty manager job would allow, she was at the legal office, helping those in need who couldn't afford legal representation. Single mothers needing enforcement of child support orders. Unlawfully evicted tenants. Well-intentioned debtors harassed by bill collectors. Even a few wrongful conviction cases. There might be no material rewards, but the knowledge that she was making a difference was better than any paycheck she had ever earned.

Maybe her love for the work stemmed in part from knowing what it felt like to be on the wrong side of things with no one in your corner. More than ever, she believed it was imperative that everyone receive a fair shake with a good lawyer behind them.

Thinking about being on the wrong side of things sent her mind whirring over all the things Rhinehardt set her up to take the fall for. It was a path she often went down, as the injustice of it was difficult to let go. Gratefully, Brad Atkins's sacrifice had paid off, his efforts exposing Rhinehardt's criminal suppression of the truth about Anavexiam and the dangers it presented. She had been called in to the U.S. Attorney's office in North Carolina more than once to give and discuss her statement, including her personal experiences with the drug in particular.

During these visits they also filled in the gaps for her, fleshing out the parts of the story she didn't know. Apparently Younger Guy was happily spilling the beans as part of a plea deal. According to him, they *had* bugged her place, which allowed them to intercept Atkins when he broke in and waited for her to return home, intending to finally confront Quinn with the truth. When Atkins tried to defend himself with a knife from Quinn's own butcher block, Younger Guy subdued him while Older Guy strangled him. Hence, no blood. They hid when Quinn came in from getting dinner at the taco truck, then—as she suggested to Shane initially—when she ran out, they carted the body down the darkened beach. Hence, no body.

According to the last update she received, the prosecutors were preparing a case with multiple charges—including kidnapping and conspiracy to murder counts for what they did to her and Ian—building a solid foundation to either force guilty pleas, or win at trial. And then there were the civil suits filed by the families of the four dead patients...

Stop.

Quinn inhaled a deep breath through her nose and blew out, letting thoughts of the Rhinehardt conspiracy drift away. She didn't need to waste one more second dwelling on it than she had to. It was in the past now. Like the events in Tampa. Like the boat when she was twelve. Like all the gossipers and whisperers and people who seemed to have a need to label her. She refused to accept those labels any longer. God defined who she was—His child, precious in His sight. And that was the only label she needed or would accept.

The parking lot for the river's launch point came up on her left. She turned in, spotted Ian's Jeep in the first row, and pulled up beside him.

"Hey, you," Ian said, coming around his unloaded kayak and gathering Quinn up in his arms, kissing her solidly before she pulled back.

"Hey, you," she said, grinning and giving him one more peck before they worked together to unload her kayak. In minutes they were on the water, cruising quietly down the first stretch.

The water, still at its year-round seventy-two degrees, was almost the same temperature as the air. There was a slight breeze, carrying the scent of the seasons changing as the bank grasses and vegetation shifted into autumn mode, browning here and there, while rust-red leaves dressed the Florida maples set back from the water's edge. The day was gorgeous, even though the sky was greyish-white and wispy with only the occasional peep of blue.

Quinn glanced over at Ian, her heart thumping harder as she eyed the man who had stolen it. He had taken up kayaking because it was her thing, but after just a few weeks he was hooked and now paddled as much or more than she did. She loved being with someone she could share this passion with.

He caught her watching him, grinned that grin that still made her heart skip—but in a good way—and dipped his paddle in again, pulling ahead of her with a wink, challenging her to keep up.

Ian's heartbeats quickened as he looked to the side and caught Quinn smiling at him. Still, after six months, one smile was all it took to get his pulse racing. The autumn sunlight was low in the sky, its rays cutting across Quinn at an angle that made her red hair glisten ruby-gold, her skin nearly luminescent, and he almost laughed at the thought that this incredible creature wanted to be with him. Just then his phone buzzed, alerting him to a text coming through. He read it and smiled.

It was on.

He dipped his paddle in the water, digging with enough force to propel him forward, knowing the competitor in Quinn would be unable to fight the urge to best him. Just to seal the deal, he winked. Sure enough, playful determination scrunched her face as she dug in harder.

As they raced along against the sound of their paddles working to beat one another, he marveled at the turn his life had taken in the year since leaving Chicago. When he moved to Seaglass Cove, he told himself it was to get a fresh start. But if he was really honest, he had to admit he came there to erase himself and, hopefully, the pain of his past. Now he knew that wasn't the answer, because doing so would mean letting go of all the good as well as the bad. He hadn't realized that until she came along. Until Quinn, he hadn't been open to trusting anyone with the truth. But now that he had, for the first time since the nightmare in Chicago he felt fully himself again—keeping the good parts, while retaining the lessons from his mistakes. He was even back in church again, attending Hope Community with Quinn. Running from his faith was one of the worst decisions he had made; coming back to it, one of the best.

His chest tightened as he saw the spot coming up on the right riverbank—the side she was on—exactly as planned. The lookout he had stationed there had seen them coming and texted he was leaving.

This is it.

His nerves lit up, sending currents of expectation through him as he pulled his paddle out of the water and pointed it at the riverbank.

I'VE GOT YOU, Quinn thought. Focusing, she plunged her paddle in again, a quarter-length from passing him, when he pulled his paddle out of the water and pointed it at the riverbank on her right.

"What is that?" he asked. Though his brow was furrowed in

curiosity, his lips were contradictorily pulled up at the corners. Suspicion tingled in her belly.

"What is what?" she asked, dragging her paddle in the water to slow her progress.

He poked his paddle at the riverbank again. "That, right there, on the bank," he replied, the corners of his mouth rising even higher as the concern lines disappeared altogether.

She followed his gaze to the edge of a small, sandy flat lined with masses of flowering pickerelweed, the plentiful, purplish-blue spikes showering the bank with color. In the midst of them, tied to one of those spikes was a giant bow made of wide white ribbon.

Quinn's pulse quickened as she looked back at Ian. His charcoal eyes held her gaze with a twinkle, as he offered a roguish shrug that said, "Beats me." But she knew him. And she knew better.

Grinning, she paddled hard over to the sand flat, beached her kayak, then waded through the clear shallow water to the edge of the pickerelweed. The bow was actually attached to the top of a stake driven into the riverbed. Behind the bow, affixed securely to the back side of the stake with heavy-duty elastic bands was a shiny gold box.

And inside the gold box, on a pillow of white satin, was the most beautiful diamond ring Quinn had ever seen.

NOTE TO MY READERS

I hope you enjoyed **LIAR LIKE HER**. If you did, please leave a review on Amazon, Goodreads, Bookbub, and whatever other social media platforms you enjoy. Reviews and word of mouth are what keep a novelist's work alive, and I would be extremely grateful for yours.

Would you like a free, award-winning short story?

Visit my website at www.dlwoodonline.com to subscribe to my newsletter, which will keep you updated (usually only twice a month) on free goodies, giveaways, new releases, discounts, advance review team opportunities and more. The short story is my free gift to you for subscribing. While you're there check out my other CleanCaptivatingFiction™ including *The Unintended Series* and *The Criminal Collection*.

FOLLOW AUTHOR D.L. WOOD

It's a tremendous help to authors when readers follow us on social media. Don't miss a thing —follow me on these platforms so you'll know about my latest releases, bargains and more. Thank you!

Facebook
https://facebook.com/dlwoodonline
Goodreads
https://www.goodreads.com/dlwood
Bookbub
https://www.bookbub.com/authors/d-l-wood
Twitter
https://www.twitter.com/dlwoodonline
Amazon
https://amazon.com/D.L.-Wood/e/B0165NBAMC
YouTube
https://youtube.com/channel/UCMYV7dogFR49f_ZobZnahOA

WANT MORE SECRETS AND LIES NOVELS?

Boston police detective Dani Lake dreads returning to her hometown of Skye, Alabama, for her 10-year high school reunion. But not for the normal reasons.

At fifteen, Dani discovered the body of her classmate, and her failure to provide evidence leading to the killer resulted in the unjust conviction of her dear friend and a guilt burden she carried for life. When new evidence is unearthed during her visit, suggesting the truth she's always suspected, she embarks on a mission to expose the killer, aided by police detective Chris Newton, who just happens to be the man Dani's best friend is dying to set her up with, and the only person who believes her.

But when Dani pushes too hard, someone pushes back, endangering Dani and those closest to her as she uncovers secrets deeper and darker than she ever expected to learn— secrets that may bring the truth to light, if they don't get her killed first.

SECRETS SHE KNEW is the first of the stand-alone *Secrets and Lies Suspense Novels.*

GET YOUR COPY AND START READING NOW

BONUS EXCERPT FROM
UNINTENDED TARGET

Have you tried D.L. Wood's *Unintended Series?* On the following pages is an excerpt from *UNINTENDED TARGET*, the first novel in this series which has captivated readers, with over 2 million pages read on Kindle Unlimited alone.

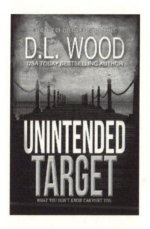

This series follows Chloe McConnaughey, an unsuspecting travel photojournalist, thrust into harrowing and mysterious circumstances ripe with murder, mayhem, and more. And by more, I mean a handsome man or two that seem too good to be true—and just might be. Turn the page to get started.

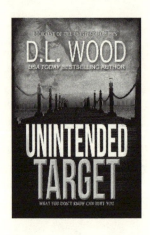

CHAPTER ONE

"He's done it again," groaned Chloe McConnaughey, her cell held to her ear by her shoulder as she pulled one final pair of shorts out of her dresser. "Tate knew that I had to leave by 3:30 at the latest. I sent him a text. I know he got it," she said, crossing her bedroom to the duffel bag sitting on her four-poster bed and tossing in the shorts.

Her best friend's voice rang sympathetically out of the phone. "There's another flight out tomorrow," offered Izzie Morales hesitantly.

Chloe zipped up the bag. "I know," she said sadly. "But, that isn't the point. As usual, it's all about Tate. It doesn't matter to him that I'm supposed to be landing on St. Gideon in six hours. What does an assignment in the Caribbean matter when your estranged brother decides it's time to finally get together?"

"Estranged is a bit of a stretch, don't you think?" Izzie asked.

"It's been three months. No texts. No calls. Nothing," Chloe replied, turning to sit on the bed.

"You know Tate. He gets like this. He doesn't mean anything by it. He just got . . . distracted," Izzie offered.

"For three months?"

Izzie changed gears. "Well, it's only 3:00—maybe he'll show."

"And we'll have, what, like thirty minutes before I have to go?" Chloe grunted in frustration. "What's the point?"

"Come on," Izzie said, "The point is, maybe this gets repaired."

Chloe sighed. "I know. I know," she said resignedly. "That's why I'm waiting it out." She paused. "He said he had news he didn't want to share over the phone. Seriously, what kind of news can't you share over the phone?"

"Maybe it's so good that he just has to tell you in person," Izzie suggested hopefully.

"Or maybe it's—'I've been fired again, and I need a place to crash.'"

"Think positively," Izzie encouraged, and Chloe heard a faint tap-tapping in the receiver. She pictured her friend on the other side of Atlanta, drumming a perfectly manicured, red-tipped finger on a nearby surface, her long, pitch-colored hair hanging in straight, silky swaths on either side of her face.

"He'll probably pull up any minute, dying to see you," Izzie urged. "And if he's late, you can reschedule your flight for tomorrow. Perk of having your boss as your best friend. I'll authorize the magazine to pay for the ticket change. Unavoidable family emergency, right?"

Chloe sighed again, picked up the duffel bag and started down the hall of her two-bedroom rental. "I just wish it wasn't this hard." The distance between them hadn't been her choice and she hated it. "Ten to one he calls to say he's had a change of plans, too busy with work, can't make it."

"He won't," replied Izzie.

With a thud, Chloe dropped the bag onto the kitchen floor by the door to the garage, trading it for half a glass of merlot perched on the counter. She took a small sip. "Don't underestimate him. His over-achievement extends to every part of his life, including his ability to disappoint."

"Ouch." Izzie paused. "You know, Chlo, it's just the job."

"I have a job. And somehow I manage to answer my calls."

"But your schedule's a little more your own, right? Pressure-wise I think he's got a little bit more to worry about."

Chloe rolled her eyes. "Nice try. But he manages tech security at an investment firm, not the White House. It's the same thing every time. He's totally consumed."

"Well, speaking as your editor, being a *little* consumed by your job is not always a bad thing."

"Ha-ha."

"What's important is that he's trying to reconnect now."

Chloe brushed at a dust bunny clinging to her white tee shirt, flicking it to the floor. "What if he really has lost this job? It took him two years after the lawsuit to find this one."

"Look, maybe it's a promotion. Maybe he got a bonus, and he's finally setting you up. Hey, maybe he's already bought you that mansion in Ansley Park..."

"I don't *need* him to set me up—I'm not eight years old anymore. I'm fine now. I wish he'd just drop the 'big-brother-takes-care-of-wounded-little-sister' thing. He's the wounded one."

"You know, if you don't lighten up a bit, it may be another three months before he comes back to see you."

"One more day and he wouldn't have caught me at all."

Izzie groaned jealously. "It's not fair that you get to go and I have to stay. It's supposed to be thirty-nine and rainy in Atlanta for, like, the next month."

"So come along."

"If only. You know I can't. Zach's got his school play next weekend. And Dan would kill me if I left him with Anna for more than a couple days right now." A squeal sounded on Izzie's end. "Uggggh. I think Anna just bit Zach again. I've gotta go. Don't forget to call me tomorrow and let me know how it went with big brother."

"Bigger by just three minutes," she quickly pointed out. "And I'll try to text you between massages in the beach-side cabana."

Izzie groaned again, drowning out another squeal in the background. "You're sick."

"It's a gift," Chloe retorted impishly before hanging up.

Chloe stared down at the duffel and, next to it, the special backpack holding her photography equipment. She double-checked the *Terra Traveler* I.D. tags on both and found all her information still legible and secure. "Now what?" she muttered.

Her stomach rumbled, reminding her that, with all the packing and preparation for leaving the house for two weeks, she had forgotten to eat. Rummaging through the fridge, she found a two-day old container of Chinese take-out. Tate absolutely hated Chinese food. She loved it. Her mouth curved at the edges as she shut the refrigerator door. *And that's the least of our differences.*

Leaning against the counter, she cracked open the container and used her chopsticks to pluck julienne carrots out of her sweet and sour chicken. *Too bad Jonah's not here,* she thought, dropping the orange slivers distastefully into the sink. *Crazy dog eats anything. Would've scarfed them down in half a second.* But the golden retriever that was her only roommate was bunking at the kennel now. She missed him already. She felt bad about leaving him for two whole weeks. Usually her trips as a travel journalist for *Terra Traveler* were much shorter, but she'd tacked on some vacation time to this one in order to do some work on her personal book project. She wished she had someone she could leave him with, but Izzie was her only close friend, and she had her hands full with her kids.

Jonah would definitely be easier than those two, she thought with a smile. He definitely had been the easiest and most dependable roommate she'd ever had—and the only male that had never let her down. A loyal friend through a bad patch of three lousy boyfriends. The last of them consumed twelve months of her life before taking her "ring-shopping," only to announce the next day that he was leaving her for his ex. It had taken six months, dozens of amateur therapy sessions with Izzie and exceeding the limit on her VISA more than once to get over that one. After that she'd sworn off men for the fore-seeable future, except for Jonah of course, which, actually, he seemed quite pleased about.

She shoveled in the last few bites of fried rice, then tossed the box into the trash. *Come to think of it,* she considered as she headed for the living room, *Tate'll be the first man to step inside this house in almost a year.* She wasn't sure whether that was empowering or pathetic.

"Not going there," she told herself, forcing her train of thought instead to the sunny beaches of St. Gideon. The all-expenses paid jaunts were the only real perks of her job as a staff journalist with *Terra Traveler,* an online travel magazine based out of Atlanta. They were also the only reason she'd stayed on for the last four years despite her abysmal pay. Photography, her real passion, had never even paid the grocery bill, much less the rent. Often times the trips offered some truly unique spots to shoot in. Odd little places like the "World's Largest Tree House," tucked away in the Smoky Mountains, or the home of the largest outdoor collection of ice sculptures in a tiny town in Iceland. And sometimes she caught a real gem, like this trip to the Caribbean. Sun, sand, and separation from everything stressful. For two whole weeks.

The thought of being stress-free reminded her that at this particular moment, she wasn't. Frustration flared as she thought of Tate's text just an hour before:

Flying in tonite. Ur place @ 2. Big news. See u then.

Typical Tate. No advance warning. No, *"I'm sorry I haven't returned a single call in three months"* or *"Surprise, I haven't fallen off the face of the earth. Wanna get together?"* Just a demand.

A familiar knot of resentment tightened in her chest as she took her wine into the living room, turned up Adele on the stereo and plopped onto a slipcovered couch facing the fire. Several dog-eared books were stacked near the armrest, and she pushed them aside to make room as she sank into the loosely stuffed cushions. She drew her favorite quilt around her, a mismatched pink and beige patchwork that melded perfectly with the hodgepodge of antique and shabby chic furnishings that filled the room.

What do you say to a brother who by all appearances has intentionally ignored you for months? It's one thing for two friends to become engrossed in their own lives and lose track of each other for a while. It's something else altogether when your twin brother doesn't return your calls. He hadn't been ill, although that had been her first thought. After the first few weeks she got a text from him saying, *sorry, so busy, talk to u ltr.* So she had called his office just to make sure he was still going in. He was. He didn't take her call that day either.

She tried to remember how many times she'd heard "big news" from Tate before, but quickly realized she'd lost count years ago. A pang of pity slipped in beside the frustration, wearing away at its edges.

She set her goblet down on the end table beside a framed picture of Tate. In many respects it might as well have been a mirror. They shared the same large amber eyes and tawny hair, though she let her loose curls grow to just below her narrow shoulders. Their oval faces and fair skin could've been photo-copied they were so similar. But he was taller and stockier, significantly out-sizing her petite, five foot four frame. She ran a finger along the faint, half-inch scar just below her chin that also differentiated them. He'd given her that in a particularly fierce game of keep-away when they were six. Later, disappointed that she had an identifying mark he didn't, he had unsuccessfully tried duplicating the scar by giving himself a nasty paper cut. In her teenage years she'd detested the thin, raised line, but now she rubbed it fondly, feeling that in some small, strange way it linked her to him.

He had broken her heart more than a little, the way he'd shut her out since taking the position at Inverse Financial nearly a year ago. He'd always been the type to throw himself completely into what he was doing, but this time he'd taken his devotion to a new high, allowing it to alienate everyone and everything in his life.

It hadn't always been that way. At least not with her. They'd grown up close, always each other's best friend and champion. Each other's only champion, really. It was how they survived the day after their eighth birthday when their father, a small-time attorney, ran off to North Carolina with the office copy lady. That was when Tate had snuck into their mother's bedroom, found a half-used box of Kleenex and brought it to Chloe as she hid behind the winter clothes in her closet. *I'll always take care of you, Chlo. Don't cry. I'm big enough to take care of both of us.* He'd said it with so much conviction that she'd believed him.

Together they'd gotten through the day nine months after that when the divorce settlement forced them out of their two-story Colonial into an orange rancher in the projects. Together they weathered their mother's alcoholism that didn't make her mean, just tragic, and finally, just dead, forcing them into foster homes. And though they didn't find any love there, they did manage to stay together for the year and a half till they turned eighteen.

Then he went to Georgia Tech on a scholarship and she, still at a loss for what she wanted to do in life, took odd jobs in the city. The teeny one bedroom apartment they shared seemed like their very own castle. After a couple of years, he convinced her she was going nowhere without a degree, so she started at the University of Georgia. For the first time they were separated. But Athens was only a couple hours away and he visited when he could and still paid for everything financial aid didn't. She'd tried to convince him she could make it on her own, but he never listened, still determined to be the provider their father had never been.

When she graduated, she moved back to Atlanta with her journalism degree under her belt and started out as a copy editor for a local events magazine. Tate got his masters in computer engineering at the same time and snagged a highly competitive job as a software designer for an up-and-coming software development company. It didn't take long for them to recognize Tate's brilliance at anything with code, and the promotions seemed to come one after the other.

Things had been so good then. They were both happy, both making money, though she was only making a little and he, more and more as time went by. The photo in her hands had been taken back then, when the world was his for the taking. Before it all fell apart for him with that one twist of fate that had ruined everything—

Stop, she told herself, shaking off the unpleasant memory. The whole episode had nearly killed Tate, and she didn't like to dwell on it. It had left him practically suicidal until, finally, this Inverse job came along. When it did, she thought that everything would get better, that things would just go back to normal. But they didn't. Instead Tate had just slowly disappeared from her life, consumed by making his career work . . .

She brushed his frozen smile with her fingers. Affection and pity and a need for the only person who had ever made her feel like she was a part of something special swelled, finally beating out the aggravation she had been indulging. As she set the frame back on the table, her phone rang.

Speak of the devil, she thought, smiling as she reached for her cell.

"Hello?"

A deep, tentative voice that did not belong to her brother answered.

* * * * *

It never ceased to amaze him how death could be so close to a person without them sensing it at all. Four hours had passed and she hadn't noticed a thing. It was dark now, and rain that was turning to sleet ticked steadily on the car, draping him in a curtain of sound as he watched her vague grey shadow float back and forth against the glow of her drawn Roman blinds. He was invisible here, hunkered down across the street behind the tinted windows of his dark Chevy Impala, swathed in the added darkness of the thick oaks lining the neighbor's yard.

Invisible eyes watching. Waiting.

Watch. Wait. Simple enough instructions. But more were coming. Out of habit he felt the Glock cradled in his jacket and fleetingly wondered *why* he was watching her, before quickly realizing he didn't care. He wasn't paid to wonder.

He was just a hired gun. A temporary fix until the big guns arrived. But, even so . . .

He scanned the yard. The dog was gone. She was completely alone. *It would be, oh, so easy.*

But he was being paid to watch. Nothing more.

Her shadow danced incessantly from one end of the room to the other. Apparently the news had her pacing.

What would she do if she knew she was one phone call away from never making a shadow dance again?

THE STORY CONTINUES IN *UNINTENDED TARGET*
GET YOUR COPY ON AMAZON NOW

ABOUT THE AUTHOR

D.L. Wood is a *USA TODAY* bestselling author who writes thrilling suspense laced with romance and faith. In her novels she tries to give readers the same thing she wants: a "can't-put-it-down-stay-up-till-3am" character-driven story, full of heart, believability, and adrenaline. Her award-winning books offer clean, captivating fiction that entertains and uplifts.

D.L. lives in North Alabama, where, if she isn't writing, you'll probably catch her curled up with a cup of Earl Grey and her Westies—Frodo and Dobby—bingeing on the latest BBC detective series. If you have one to recommend, please email her immediately, because she's nearly exhausted the ones she knows about. She loves to hear from readers, and you can reach her at dlwood@dlwoodonline.com.

BOOKS BY D.L. WOOD

THE UNINTENDED SERIES

Unintended Target

Unintended Witness

Unintended Detour

THE CRIMINAL COLLECTION

A Criminal Game

BOOK TWO: COMING SOON

THE SECRETS AND LIES SUSPENSE NOVELS

Secrets She Knew

Liar Like Her

Manufactured by Amazon.ca
Bolton, ON